se

Leaving the Log House

AINSLIE MANSON

ORCA BOOK PUBLISHERS

National Library of Canada Cataloguing in Publication Data
Manson, Ainslie
   Leaving the log house / Ainslie Manson
ISBN 1-55143-258-7
I. Title.
PS8576.A567L42 2003   jC813'.54   C2002-911451-9
PZ7.M31813Le 2003

First published in the United States, 2003

Library of Congress Control Number: 2002116157

Summary: Two small, fragile dolls help Teresa cope as she gets her first
prosthetic leg in a city far from home.

Free teachers' guide available.

Orca Book Publishers gratefully acknowledges the support for its publishing
programs provided by the following agencies: the Government of Canada
through the Book Publishing Industry Development Program (BPIDP), the
Canada Council for the Arts, and the British Columbia Arts Council.

Cover illustration by Ron Lightburn
Cover design by Christine Toller
Printed and bound in Canada

IN CANADA: **IN THE UNITED STATES:**
Orca Book Publishers   **Orca Book Publishers**
1030 North Park Street   PO Box 468
Victoria, BC Canada   Custer, WA USA
V8T 1C6   98240-0468

05 04 03 • 5 4 3 2

Because he's never forgotten Tape and Curly, I dedicate this book to my brother Kim.

Leaving the Log House

"Are they still waving?" Teresa asked her brother.

Tom nodded. The plane picked up speed. Tom was by the window; he could see them. Teresa tried to picture Mum, Dad, Janette and baby John growing smaller and smaller. Baby John was still too young to wave. He would be the bundle Mum was carrying in her arms.

The plane's belly growled. It sounded like she felt. She wrapped her arms around her middle and rocked back and forth.

The flight attendant had ignored her. "We'll put your sister in the aisle seat," she had said to Tom. "It will be more convenient for her."

Teresa scowled. She could easily have wiggled her way across to the window. They'd even given her a blanket, like she was sick or something. Why hadn't she spoken up?

She wished Mum had come. She had said she couldn't because of baby John. Mum had felt he might catch something in the hospital waiting room. Teresa knew it wasn't like that. People didn't get sick when they went to hospitals. They went there to get well. Or sometimes, like her, they went there to get a leg.

"Can you still see them, Tom?"

Tom shook his head, his nose still pressed against the windowpane. "Not now."

Teresa stared at the seat in front of her and sighed. "At least you saw them," she said. "From this seat I can't see a thing."

"Don't blame me! It's not my fault that she put me by the window," Tom said.

"We could share …" Teresa suggested.

"No we couldn't," said Tom. "We're supposed to stay buckled up, Twig."

The rest of her family called her Tree, short for Teresa, but Tom called her Twig. He said she had a lot of growing to do before she'd be a tree. Teresa couldn't see his face, but she knew he was gloating. She'd hoped that flying with Tom would be fun.

From her seat, she could see the tops of trees on either side of the runway. They were becoming blurry now. The plane sped along, faster and faster. She wasn't afraid, but she did wish she could hold Tom's hand, just while they were taking off. Under cover of her blanket, she reached for his sleeve. The plane lifted. Up, up they went, into a cloudy sky. Teresa squeezed as hard as she could.

"Ouch, Twig!" Tom said.

"Oh, sorry." She crossed her arms.

As the plane leveled out, she felt a little better. She pointed her toe and admired her new pink runner. Its mate was in her suitcase. Soon she'd use it, too.

They were leaving the small Anahim airfield behind. They were leaving home behind. She swung her leg, back and forth, back and forth, kicking the seat in front of her as she thought about it. A man with thick, frowning eyebrows peered back at her between the seats. Luckily Tom didn't see him; he'd have bawled her out for sure.

Tom was going to stay with her in Vancouver, but just for a few nights. Then he had a job helping a friend of Dad, who had a farm out in the valley. He lived alone. His wife had died and his kids had grown up and moved away. Tom would work full-time with Dad's friend for the summer and then just part-time when school started. The school where he was going wasn't too far from the farm, and they played a lot of hockey there. Tom loved hockey and he was smart in school. His teacher at home said he had learned as much as he could at the village school and it was time to move on.

She wondered how long she'd have to stay with the Mullans. Months and months? She gave Tom a poke to raise him from his window-gazing daydreams.

"Tom, how long will it take?"

"How long will *what* take?"

Teresa ignored the grumble in his voice. At least he had turned from the window.

"How long will it take for me to learn how to walk on my new leg?"

Tom shrugged. "I guess it depends on how hard you work at it, Twig."

"Well, say I work at it really, really hard. Say I hardly sleep, I work so hard."

"Then I bet you'll be faster than anyone has ever been since the invention of the first wooden leg! You'll set new-leg walking records!"

It wasn't really an answer, and his voice had a teasing tone to it, but still his words did chuff her up a little.

She tried to visualize herself racing down the hospital corridor on her new leg, but she couldn't. "I wish I could remember the hospital better, Tom. What's it like there?"

"I don't know, Twig. You're the one who's been there, not me. All I can remember is you going. You and Mum got to go in a helicopter, and I had to stay home. Boy, was I jealous!" Tom shook his head and chuckled. "Worse still, Mum took Janette in that helicopter, and she was only a baby then, like John is now."

Teresa frowned. "If Janette came down to the city when she was a baby, why couldn't Mum have brought baby John this time?"

Tom turned his back again. "You know why, Twig. John gets sick too easily. And what about Janette? Who'd look after her if Mum took off?

Teresa slumped lower in her seat. Why couldn't Dad stay home with Janette? But of course he wasn't there much. He was always off working or trying to find work, either in the bush or on boats.

Mum and Dad would be in the truck now. They'd be getting groceries in Anahim and then heading home to the log house. She thought about her dog, Clifford. He'd be waiting for them, waiting for *her*, at the gate. He'd prance around and wag his tail when he saw the truck coming back. Would he be disappointed when she didn't hop out? Would he miss her as much as she'd miss him? Last night she'd let him onto her bed and she'd cried into his fur.

She squeezed her eyes tight shut. What had Mrs. Skiffany, the district nurse, said? "Teresa, go for it! You can do it. You've got the courage of a lion!"

"Me? What do you mean?" Teresa had asked. She didn't think she was brave at all.

"You've never been afraid to try anything new, Teresa. And I think you'll regret it if you don't try this."

Mrs. Skiffany's words had made her feel tall and fearless — but that was then. What was it going to be like? How much courage would she really need?

Whenever she tried to remember walking and running on two legs, the crutches always crept into the picture. She had only been three years old when Tom had taken her for a ride on the back of Dad's all-terrain vehicle and they'd rolled into a ditch. Probably because of that, Dad hadn't ever let Tom on an ATV again. Not even on the back. Tom hated that.

It seemed so strange that she couldn't remember anything from before the accident. Mum said no one remembered things from when they were that little. But it must have hurt so much when the ATV rolled right over her leg. You'd think she'd at least remember that.

In the hospital they'd made her sleep in a crib. That was her very first memory. It had made her feel like a baby. But she hadn't minded that as much as she'd minded the nights, when Mum had left. Mum had stayed with the Mullans, just like she and Tom were going to now. Auntie Bee Mullan was Mum's sister, and she'd helped out by looking after Janette so that Mum could be with Teresa without a baby to worry about.

Teresa hadn't liked her little sister much back then. But now she loved her more than anyone in the world. They slept side by side in the loft, and when Janette had a bad dream, she called for Teresa, not for Mum.

Only baby John got to sleep in Mum and Dad's room downstairs.

"Tom, just think," she said, "Janette will be all alone in the loft with us gone."

Tom laughed. "Lucky Janette!" he said. "I sure hope I have a room of my own at Max Solesky's farm!"

Teresa closed her eyes. Tom didn't understand. Janette would miss her. But as she had pointed out to her little sister, there was a good side to the missing, too. When Teresa got back, they'd be able to do lots of things together that they'd never been able to do before. They'd run races and they'd ride the neighbor's horses and they'd even learn to skate! They'd go down to the lake when it was windy, and they'd hold out their coats, and they'd fly, fly across the ice. Teresa had seen Tom doing that with his friends and it looked like more fun than anything.

She'd play hockey, too. She'd be right out there on the ice with Tom and the other kids from school. Up till now, she'd only been able to watch their games. Maybe she'd be the goalie. The rumbling engine acted as a lullaby. With visions of flying pucks she drifted off to dreamland.

A bump woke her as the plane touched down. When she opened her eyes, there was Tom, with his nose still pressed against the windowpane. It couldn't have been a very long flight. As far as she knew, they hadn't even brought juice.

Tom turned to her. "Too bad you were asleep when we were coming in. We swooped in over the mountains and banked over the sea. Vancouver looked awesome from up there. And look! The sun is shining."

Teresa turned her head away. Out the window across the aisle she could see the airport buildings now. As the plane bumped along the tarmac, the buildings grew larger and became more daunting.

2.
The City

Vancouver airport was crowded. Teresa had never seen so many people. They were racing, rushing, bumping, shoving and never saying excuse me.

"How will we ever find Auntie Bee, Tom? We don't even know what she looks like!"

"Don't be stupid. Of course we do!"

Then she remembered. Tom knew what she looked like. He'd stayed overnight with the Mullans when he'd come down with Dad to check out Max's farm and the school.

"There she is!" Tom waved. "I see her! She said she'd be wearing a red hat, and she is."

All Teresa could see were feet and legs and backsides. She was too low down. She'd wanted to use her crutches, but the flight attendant had insisted on a wheelchair.

People streamed around them as Auntie Bee rushed up and greeted them with hugs and kisses. Teresa stared at her unfamiliar face. She acted as though they'd all been together just a few weeks before … but they hadn't. She was like a total stranger.

"Tom, you're as tall as I am!" she said.

Teresa sat up as straight as she could. Lately she'd been growing faster than Tom.

"And Teresa! Look at you. Oh my goodness, you are *so* like your mother."

Teresa tried a smile, but it felt stiff and forced like a television toothpaste commercial. She did have dark hair and dark eyes like her mother, but that was all.

At the luggage carousel, she switched to her crutches. It took two carts to haul all the suitcases to the car. Tom pushed one, Auntie Bee the other. Teresa followed behind. The car was a station wagon. While Tom and Auntie Bee were busy packing everything into the far back, Teresa climbed into the backseat. Tom could sit in the front and answer all the questions.

As they drove through the noisy, busy city, she studied Auntie Bee's profile. She was turned towards Tom, saying something and smiling, and Teresa noticed a dimple, just like Mum's, in her right cheek. She also had that funny way of tilting her head as she listened. She was the one who looked like Mum. Teresa closed her eyes, wishing hard that Auntie Bee would suddenly become Mum. But she didn't. An unfamiliar ache moved slowly down her throat and settled somewhere near her heart.

Cars honked and brakes screeched. People hurried along the cement sidewalks, dodging one another and dodging cars as they crossed streets. Everything was racing, but Auntie Bee didn't seem the least bit disturbed. She turned left, then right, then right again, weaving in and out between huge buses and trucks.

Teresa was relieved when they finally came to a full stop. Auntie Bee turned off the ignition.

"We're here," she said. "Does it look familiar?"

Teresa shook her head. The house sat almost on the sidewalk. There was no garden in front of it, just a strip of tired grass on either side of the front door.

"Sure it does," said Tom. But he'd seen it recently.

Teresa liked the inside better. The living room was the kind you could curl up in. A black-and-white cat had chosen the best curling-up spot though — a basket chair that looked like a large nest.

Auntie Bee helped her carry her suitcases upstairs.

"Right in here, Teresa," she said.

The room was bright. It had flowered wallpaper and the sun shone in through an open window. The yellow striped curtains matched the bedspreads on the two beds. It was pretty, but it seemed empty compared to their crowded loft at home. She was glad Tom would be sharing it with her, at least for the first few nights.

"Why don't you unpack and put a few things away?" Auntie Bee suggested. "The bathroom's just down the hall if you want a wash."

"Where, Tom?" Teresa whispered when they were left alone.

Tom shrugged. "Just down the hall like she said. You'll find it." He tossed his knapsack onto the bed. "I'll unpack later. Or maybe I won't bother. I'm only going to be here a few nights."

Tom left and Teresa's heart sank. She made her way cautiously down the hall to the bathroom. Wash? Did Auntie Bee mean she should have a bath? She looked at the neatly piled towels. Which one would she use if she had a bath? She went back to her room and sank down onto the bed that didn't have Tom's knapsack on it.

"Teresa!" It was Auntie Bee calling from downstairs. "Why don't you come on down and have a sandwich? You must be starved."

Teresa took a deep breath and then, trying hard to keep her voice steady, she called back, "I … I'm not very hungry. I'm just tired. I think I'll … I'll just have a nap."

Auntie Bee took the stairs two at a time and was at the door before Teresa could compose herself.

"Are you sure you're not hungry?"

Teresa nodded and turned away. She could feel the tears welling up.

"Suit yourself," said Auntie Bee. "Have a short nap, but then you'd better come down because you'll have to eat something."

Much to Teresa's relief, she left the room right away, closing the door behind her.

Teresa folded back the yellow-and-white striped bedspread. If she got it all crinkled, Auntie Bee might get mad. She flopped down on the less new-looking striped blanket underneath and buried her face in the pillow. Her sobs almost choked her as she struggled to keep them quiet. What on earth was she doing here, so far away from Mum and Dad and Janette? And Tom was being so mean! He didn't care about her one bit. He only cared about himself.

Teresa stayed in her room all afternoon. She cried a lot, slept a little, but mostly she lay still and thought about what would happen next. She knew she wanted the leg, but if only she could just snap her fingers and it would be there. Was it going to hurt? The district nurse had said it wouldn't, but was she just saying that? It had sounded so easy, almost like it would be fun, but now it just seemed scary.

Auntie Bee came to check on her a few times. But whenever Teresa heard her footstep on the stairs, she turned her face to the wall and pretended she was asleep. She was glad Tom didn't come. He'd have looked at her puffy, red eyes and called her a baby.

When Auntie Bee tiptoed back downstairs after a

third checkup, Teresa took a deep breath, sat up and made a closer study of the room that would be hers for the next few weeks … or months.

The leafy tree right outside the window made dancing shadows on the floor. Birds chirped in the tree, but as well as their familiar sound there was a constant hum of city traffic.

She reached for her crutches and made her way over to the window. At home she couldn't see a single neighbor from the windows, but here she could see one on either side and at least eight across the street. Did Auntie Bee and Uncle Edward know all these people? Were they friends? Did they borrow things from each other, like cups of sugar?

Only an occasional car passed below her, but a few people sat on their steps, and a few more worked in the small grassy patches by their front doors.

As Teresa rested her elbows on the sill, a man came around the corner at the end of the block. When he was right below her, he reached into his pocket and drew out a key. She looked straight down at the top of his head. He had frizzy, sticking-out hair like a bird's nest, and a pink bald spot just the shape of a large egg! She suppressed a giggle … this had to be Uncle Edward.

Just before he disappeared under the little roof that sheltered the front door, he looked up and gave her a quick smile and a wave.

The door slammed. "Calling all nieces and neph-ews!" he shouted.

"Uncle Edward!" Tom called from somewhere.

Teresa peeked through the banisters. She could just see the corner of the basket chair with Tom in it. She watched as he jumped up, dropped the cat and ran to the door. Tom and Uncle Edward greeted each other in the boy way, with "high fives" and shoulder hugs.

Then Uncle Edward saw her watching and he grinned at her.

"That really was you, was it, Teresa? Looking down from your garret window? It's wonderful to see you again after so long!"

He didn't wait for her answer, but came bounding up the stairs and lifted her into his arms. When her crutches got in the way, he called down to Tom, "Bring the crutches, will you please, Tom?" To Teresa's sur-prise, Tom hurried up the stairs without a complaint.

It was okay being carried down the stairs by Uncle Edward. He made it like a walking hug. "I'm so glad you're going to be staying with us for awhile," he said, weaving his way through the living room and past the cat that was now back in its chair.

They all sat down around the small kitchen table. After a few minutes, when conversation seemed to be winding down, Auntie Bee mouthed the word "Now?" to Uncle Edward. He nodded and sprang to his feet.

"Oh!" he said. "I almost forgot. I have something for you, Teresa."

He went through a door at the back of the kitchen, and she heard him clatter down some stairs. He was back in a flash with an armful of logs. No, it was a house!

He set it down in the center of the kitchen table. It was a log house, so much like her own home she wondered if he could be a magician. Teresa was spell-bound. Had he shrunk her house and brought it here? Would her family suddenly burst out the front door, all finger sized?

"It is *so* cool!" said Tom. "What do you *say*, Teresa?"

He sounded like Mum or Dad. She gave him her most withering look and then turned to Uncle Edward. "You mean it's for me?" she asked.

Uncle Edward nodded. "Your dad and I built it as a model before we built your house up north," he said. "I just redesigned it a little so you could play with it more easily."

He pulled out a chair for her at the open back of the house and sat down across from her at the front. She could see one of his big brown eyes peering in the miniature kitchen window. Then his enormous hand opened the red front door. He was like a giant, but not a scary giant.

His fat fingers tried to walk inside, but they

wouldn't fit. "I took the back wall off," he explained in a voice not at all like a giant's voice, "because if I hadn't, you'd have had a hard time playing with it."

Teresa smiled.

"We'll find something to use as furniture tomorrow," said Auntie Bee. "And though I can't think where they are right now, I know I have a few small people somewhere, but I'm not going to look for them now. We have to eat while it's hot. Teresa, you must be starving."

Teresa forced a weak smile. If she'd had a choice, she'd have skipped dinner completely and just played with the log house. But her uncle took it off the table and put it at the foot of the stairs. During the meal, Teresa kept checking over her shoulder to make sure it was real.

She tried to hide her meat under a lettuce leaf, but Tom saw and nudged her.

"Eat!" he said. The others didn't seem to notice or care, so she ignored him. Eventually her plate left the table looking almost as it had when the meal began.

"It's going to be an early start in the morning," Auntie Bee announced after dinner. Then right away it was bedtime. Tom carried the log house upstairs for her. He set it down on a little table by the window.

Once she woke in the night. She wondered where she was, but then Tom snored his old familiar snore.

Light from the street shone in the window, lighting up the log house. It was as though she was looking down on her own home from the top of Caribou Hill, and those were rays of moonlight, not streetlight, reflecting on the windows.

"Goodnight, Mum and Dad," she whispered. "Goodnight, Janette and baby John. Goodnight, Clifford."

3.
The Hospital

Teresa still wasn't hungry at breakfast. She nibbled on orange segments and stared out the window. Yesterday the sun had shone, but today it was gray and raining. She tried not to listen to Tom's munching and slurping as he attacked greasy bacon and eggs and a mountain of toast.

This was the day she was going to the hospital. Would she see her new leg right away? Was it there now, waiting for her? Would she get to take it home?

"You'd better eat something, Teresa," said Auntie Bee, handing her a piece of toast. "Today's your big day. You'll need your strength."

Teresa forced a smile. "I'm just not hungry," she said.

"At least try to eat," said Tom with his mouth full.

Auntie Bee had started to leave the kitchen, but she came back. "I almost forgot," she said, grabbing something off the windowsill. "I found these for your dolls' house." Beside the toast plate she placed two small, bare, doll people.

Teresa said thank-you before Tom could jump in and remind her of her manners again.

She picked the dolls up and inspected them closely. They were unlike any she'd ever seen. One had golden brown skin. The other was bright pink. The brown-skinned doll had brown hair painted on its head. The pink one was slightly smaller and thinner and had no hair. Their limbs weren't movable; they were molded tightly to their bodies.

Their right arms were bent at their elbows and curved up towards their mouths. Their left arms were folded across their middles. Perhaps their tummies were gurgling, like Teresa's was, and they were trying to stop them.

"They're a bit strange looking," said Auntie Bee. "But they've been around a long time."

"I like them," said Teresa.

Over Teresa's shoulder, Tom examined them too. "They look like they're sucking their thumbs," he said. Then in a voice just loud enough for Teresa to hear, he added, "They're babies, Teresa, just like you."

"I like them," said Teresa again.

Tom ignored her and directed a polite, interested

smile at Auntie Bee. "What are they made of? Are they a kind of plastic?"

"I think they're actually Bakelite," said Auntie Bee. "That was a kind of early plastic."

"Long, long ago?" Teresa asked.

"Yes, quite long ago," said Auntie Bee. "They were your grandmother's when she was a child."

Teresa rolled them back and forth in her hand. Her grandmother had died when she was three. "If they were Gran's when she was a girl, they must be very old," she said.

Then, to her utter dismay, the pink one fell into two pieces. Teresa stared in horror at the hollow back and front. It must have been trying to hold itself together with its tiny bent left arm.

She thought Auntie Bee might be mad, but she didn't seem to be. She just pointed at the poor doll and laughed. "Oh, too bad," she said. "One's falling to bits!" She glanced at the kitchen clock. "We have to be on our way, Teresa. You've got an early appointment."

No sense in asking if they could fix the broken doll first. Auntie Bee was racing around the kitchen, trying to tidy up. Teresa didn't even have time to take the doll people upstairs and show them their new house, so she slipped the two of them into her jacket pockets.

She was glad to see that Tom was coming to the

hospital too. At least she'd have someone with her that she knew. This time Tom scrambled into the backseat before Teresa had a chance, so she sat up front with Auntie Bee. The traffic was terrible and Auntie Bee did a lot of sighing.

"I should have left earlier," she mumbled. "We'll never make it on time." As she wove in and out of the traffic, Teresa tried to follow her chatter.

"The hospital is in the middle of a huge renovation, so it's a bit of a mess at the moment. Oh, why does that car have to turn left now? I've met the prosthetist before … he's a nice man. And I've met Jan before, too …"

Teresa nodded, but didn't have the faintest idea what her aunt was talking about. The weaving in and out and the noise and the smells of the city were making her feel ill.

"Jan will be your … ah, there, finally, we're rid of *that* car. As I was saying … Oh dear, now I've forgotten. What was I saying?"

"I'm not … quite sure," said Teresa, wrapping her left arm around her aching stomach rather in the way the doll people did.

Tom gave a snort from the backseat. Auntie Bee's nattering was funny, but Teresa was feeling too miserable to be amused.

She felt a mixture of relief and terror when they pulled up in front of the hospital. Tom waited with her at the front door while Auntie Bee parked the car. As he babbled on about a classy car that had just pulled up to the door, Teresa took the doll people from her pockets and held them one in each hand. Managing the crutches with her thumb and index finger wrapped firmly around the pink person's wobbly body was awkward, but she didn't mind. She liked the way they felt in her hands.

Auntie Bee appeared and bustled them inside. She was out of breath and kept glancing at her watch.

"This way, this way," she said, ushering them across the entrance hall to an elevator.

"I've never been in one of these before," Teresa whispered to Tom as the door closed.

"Of course you have, Twig," said Tom. "They have them in Williams Lake, and you've been there often enough. Elevators are cool."

Teresa gave him a tentative nod. *Cool* was not the word she would have chosen. She still felt strange from the wild drive with Auntie Bee. Now each time the elevator stopped, her insides did cartwheels.

"I'll run ahead and let them know we're here," Auntie Bee said when they got off at the sixth floor. "You two follow. The waiting room is through those glass doors at the end of the hall."

Trolleys and empty beds slowed them down. And Teresa had to make her way carefully across a wet patch where a man was washing the floor.

"She should have worn that red hat again," said Tom, trying to keep an eye on Auntie Bee's progress.

Teresa came to a sudden stop when they reached the glass doors. Tom bumped her from behind, nearly tumbling her over.

The room was packed with people. Heads turned and eyes stared.

"Come on, Twig, move it," said Tom.

Teresa wanted to tell him that she'd changed her mind. Her head was spinning. She'd always managed perfectly well with one leg. Why had she come? This was a horrible place.

Tom pushed past her. "I'll find seats," he said and was gone.

Maybe she could explain to Auntie Bee. But it was too late. She was on the other side of the room, deep in conversation with a woman in white. Any minute now they'd probably come in with the leg. Would they carry it in a box, or would they cradle it in their arms like baby John.

Lots of children were sitting, waiting. She could see what some of them were waiting for. With others, it was harder to tell.

A few toys were heaped in one corner, but no one was playing with them. A table in the middle of the room was piled high with grown-up magazines. One little boy made *rum-rum* car sounds as he rested his head on the edge of the table and steered a Matchbox car through magazine tunnels. Most of the children stayed close to their parents and stared at one another.

Tom beckoned. He'd found a chair. Teresa took a big breath and maneuvered her way across the room to him. Auntie Bee joined them. She had a lady with her. The lady was pushing an empty wheelchair. There was no sign of a new leg.

Teresa scowled at the chair and stood tall and straight on her crutches.

"Teresa, this is Jan," said Auntie Bee. "She's a Child Life Worker."

Teresa wanted to ask what that meant, but she couldn't seem to find her voice.

"Sort of like your helper," said Jan. She seemed to realize that Teresa was puzzled. She went on to explain that she would be spending lots of time with her every day, taking her to meet the people she had to meet: a doctor, a prosthetist, a physiotherapist.

Teresa knew what a doctor was but had no idea about the other two.

"Teresa," said Auntie Bee, "like I explained to you in the car, Tom and I have to go now."

Go? Teresa stared at her in bewilderment. Jan was helping her off with her jacket, and she was trying to keep her balance and not drop the dolls. Now she reeled.

"I thought I'd have longer with you," said Auntie Bee. "But that traffic … and now I'm late for work.

And I've got to drop Tom at a store where he can get some boots for his farm job."

These were unexpected good-byes! Teresa glanced around the room, wishing without much hope that her mother would appear like a fairy godmother.

Auntie Bee gave her shoulder a squeeze and patted her on the back as though she were a puppy.

"I'll be back to pick you up this afternoon, Teresa." With a final, apologetic wave, she headed for the door. Tom hurried after her, not even turning to say good-bye.

Teresa's crutches clattered to the floor as she sank down into the chair that Tom had found. She stared down at her lap. A doll's face peeked out from each of her tightly clenched fists. At least they hadn't deserted her.

4.

Tape and Curly

When Teresa had recovered from the shock of Tom and Auntie Bee's departure, she realized that Jan was pointing at her clenched fists.

"What have you got there, Teresa?" She had a kind, gentle voice and the broadest smile Teresa had ever seen. It stretched right across her face.

Teresa held out her hands and the pink doll promptly fell into two pieces again. "One has a problem," she whispered.

"Well, he's come to the right place," said Jan. "I think we'd better attend to him first, don't you?"

Teresa nodded and handed him over.

Jan reached into her pocket and brought out a roll of tape and a pair of scissors. Teresa studied her while she measured and cut. She whistled while she worked, like the seven dwarfs in *Snow White*. But she wasn't little like a dwarf; she was tall and thin.

Several of the other children had crowded in close to watch. Jan knew them all by name. As she worked she answered their questions, grinned her enormous grin and explained what she was doing.

"First of all, one finger on his chest, one on his back, we make sure his two halves are truly lined up. Ah, there. Then we hold the tape like this …"

She wound a piece of white tape around the doll's middle. When the task was completed, Jan handed him back and Teresa held him up for inspection.

A boy next to her chuckled. "It looks a whole lot better than it did as two bare-naked halves," he said. "It's just like new now. They're pretty good at fixing stuff around here."

"*We* can say that 'cause *we* know, right, Carlos?" said a little girl whose right arm ended above the elbow.

Teresa took a closer look at Carlos as she pretended to study a picture on the wall right behind him. He walked with a bit of a limp, but he was wearing regular runners and socks. Were his legs his own under his jeans? Were they the flesh-and-blood kind or the other kind?

Carlos caught her staring. He grinned. Then with clenched fists he tapped both his legs below his knees. It sounded like he was knocking on a door!

"Do you think your new leg will make such great music?" he asked her.

Teresa shrugged.

"Do the dolls have names, Teresa?" Jan asked.

Teresa walked the mended doll person out along the arm of her chair. "This one is a boy, and his name is Tape," she said without hesitation.

"An appropriate name," said Carlos. "And what about the other guy? Does he have a name, too?"

"The other one is not a guy," said Teresa, looking down at the doll with the painted hair. "She's a girl and her name is Curly."

"Great name choices," said Jan, bouncing to her feet. "And now it's Teresa's turn for attention. Carlos, shouldn't you be at physio?"

Carlos nodded.

Jan turned to Teresa. "Shall we use the wheelchair, or would you prefer to walk?"

Teresa frowned at the wheelchair.

Jan nodded. "Right. Come on then. I'll lead the way."

Clutching Tape firmly in one hand, Curly in the other, Teresa swung along beside Jan.

"Why were there so many people in there?" she asked, as they went back through the glass doors.

"It's almost always like that these days," said Jan. "It's because there's only one waiting room on each floor while the renovations are going on. Lots of different departments share this one. It gets pretty crazy, but in a few years we'll have such a fabulous facility, we won't know what hit us. We'll have a huge waiting room, all to ourselves. We'll probably echo around in all the empty space!"

"Are we going to see my new leg now?" Teresa asked.

"No," said Jan. "But you're going to hear all about it. Today is casting day, so we'll be starting to build it."

"Casting day?" Teresa asked. "What does that mean?"

"Aha!" said Jan. "You're about to find out." She opened the door into a quieter, smaller room. A man in a white coat sat behind a desk. Jan made introductions. She even introduced Tape and Curly. The man's name was Robert. He'd been expecting them.

"I'm a prosthetist," he explained, "the person who will design, make and fit your new leg."

Teresa and Jan sat down in two large, low chairs. This time Teresa made sure her crutches didn't crash to the floor. She laid them down beside her. Then, still holding the doll people firmly, one in each hand, she sat up straight so she could see more than just Robert's head behind his enormous desk.

"Making a cast will be our first step," Robert continued. "Have you ever known anyone with a broken arm or leg, Teresa?"

Teresa rubbed her thumbs back and forth, back and forth on the dolls' backs. Then she nodded. "Yes," she said. "Once Tom broke his leg, and another time he broke his wrist."

"Tom is your brother?" Jan asked. "The one I met just now in the waiting room?"

Teresa nodded again.

"And did Tom have casts made both times?" Robert asked.

"Yes," said Teresa.

"Well, we're going to make you a temporary cast for your residual limb, probably much like Tom's casts," said Robert.

When Jan noticed Teresa's puzzled expression, she added, "Your residual limb is what we old professionals call your little leg or your stump."

"Oh," said Teresa.

Robert explained that her cast would only stay on until it was set or dried. Then it would be removed.

"It'll be off by lunchtime," said Jan.

"Then it will become the mold that I'll use to design and make the top part of your new leg," said Robert. "It'll be the socket for your residual limb."

"Like a pocket?" Teresa asked.

"Yes, just like a pocket," said Robert. "And now we'll measure you before we get started."

"Why?" Teresa asked Jan when Robert left the room to get the measuring tape.

"Because you're a growing girl!" said Jan. "And we're going to have to keep making adjustments to your new leg as you grow."

Teresa tried to imagine herself as a teenager with long, tanned, matching legs. Would one tan and the other stay white?

She was worried that the casting might hurt. But it didn't. She even helped Robert. She took the doll people both in one hand so that she could hand him things off a tray as he needed them. It was kind of like being his assistant.

As he wrapped her stump with plaster-of-Paris bandages, Robert told them about the trip he had made to the Vancouver Aquarium on the weekend.

"Did you see the baby beluga?" Jan asked.

"Of course," said Robert. "That's why I went. I took my son. Now he wants to rename our dog Beluga, because he's sort of that color.

"What's his name now?" Teresa asked.

"Cast," said Robert.

"Cast? You're teasing us!" said Jan.

Robert looked up from his work and laughed. "No, I promise I'm not teasing. Several years ago I rescued Cast from a horrible leg-hold trap up-country. I made a cast for his broken leg. But his cast wasn't like yours, Teresa. It was more like one of Tom's. He wore it while his leg was healing, and he didn't get a whole new leg like you're getting."

"My dog is called Clifford," said Teresa. "He's a Border collie. He's super smart and really handsome."

Thinking about Clifford made tears come to her eyes. She hurriedly wiped them away.

Jan gave Teresa's doll-free hand an encouraging squeeze. "I have a dog too," she said. "Her name is Calla, short for Callista, which means 'most beautiful' in Greek."

"Three 'C' dogs!" said Robert. "What a team! But our dog, Cast, isn't beautiful or handsome. He's loving and he's gentle, but he's motley and ugly."

They all laughed, even Teresa.

Just like Jan had said, it didn't take long for the cast to set. Then Robert explained that they would have to cut it off.

"Cut?" Teresa asked, sitting bolt upright. She had been feeling much more relaxed about the casting, but now she pictured long, sharp knives that just might slip. She clutched Tape and Curly firmly, one in each hand again.

"It's only the noise of the saw you won't like," said Robert.

Teresa swung around to see what he was holding. "It's a gentle little saw we use," he said reassuringly.

"It's still a saw!" said Teresa. "Saws are dangerous."

"Not this one," said Robert. "We have never, ever cut anybody's skin … just their casts."

Teresa wanted to believe him, but her heart was beating so hard and fast she felt it was going to burst.

"Don't worry," said Jan, patting the hand that held Tape. "It won't take long and I promise it won't hurt."

"When we've cut this little cast into two halves," Robert went on, "we'll use the halves as a model or form to make the top section of your new leg, the bit that your stump or 'little leg' will fit into."

"The socket, right?" said Teresa as the noise of the saw began.

"Exactly," said Robert. "You catch on fast!"

Just as Jan had predicted, the sawing didn't hurt and it didn't take long. It was all over by lunchtime.

"You did well!" said Jan as they headed to the cafeteria. "The first step always seems scary and hard. It will get easier. You'll see."

They had lunch with several of the other children. Tape and Curly stayed in Teresa's pockets while she ate.

Teresa sipped a bowl of soup and ate a few crackers. The little girl she'd seen earlier, whose name was Betty, proudly displayed her new prosthesis.

She held out her arm to Teresa. "You didn't see it before because it was being adjusted," she explained. Her lower arm had a colorful "Littlest Mermaid" pattern all over it.

"I got to choose," she said proudly. "I could have had almost any design at all. But I liked the Littlest

Mermaid best. Next time I might choose rabbits."

"Rabbits?" Teresa asked. "Why?"

Betty shrugged. "Because they're fuzzy and cute."

Exactly the sort of answer Janette would give, Teresa thought. And Betty was just about her sister's age ... what would Janette be doing right now? Would Mum have braided her hair for her this morning? That was always Teresa's job, and Janette liked the way she did it. Would Mum be hurried and pull too hard? Would Janette say, "You're making my eyes go all squinchy!" and start to cry?

Teresa felt an empty feeling, almost like hunger, even though she'd just eaten. She reached into her pockets and found Tape and Curly again.

"What about your leg, Teresa?" Betty asked. "Do you want pictures too?"

Teresa shrugged. Until now she'd been hoping that the new leg would look exactly like a real leg. Then people like that flight attendant on the plane wouldn't even be able to tell.

"Does everyone get to choose like Betty did?" she asked Jan. "Will I get to choose too?"

Jan grinned. "Absolutely," she said. "Not with this first prosthesis, which is like a test leg and will be a clear plastic, but in a few months you'll be allowed to choose whatever design you like."

"Or no design at all," said Carlos from across the table. He'd just arrived with a heap of food like Tom would eat. "My legs are more like Terry Fox's leg was." He raised his pant legs and Teresa stared incredulously at two metal posts.

"A lot to think about, right?" said Jan as she and Teresa returned to the waiting room to meet Auntie Bee. "Busy days ahead. You've the weekend off now, but on Monday we'll give you your timetable. Then you'll be able to keep track of all your appointments. We'll be squeezing in as much school time as possible, too."

"School? But it's summer," said Teresa.

Jan laughed. "Because no one can spend all day in this classroom, we keep our school going all summer long," she explained. "That way our kids don't get behind in their schoolwork. You'll meet your teacher on Monday, Teresa."

Teresa and Auntie Bee got home before the others. Teresa didn't feel like talking about her day just yet. Fortunately, Auntie Bee didn't seem to mind her silence. Teresa stared with envy at the black-and-white cat in the basket chair. She felt too tired to climb the stairs.

"His name is Bobby Sox," Auntie Bee said. "I'm sure he wouldn't mind you sharing his chair."

Teresa nodded, climbed into the chair and took the cat on her knee. Curly and Tape were in her jeans' pockets. She guessed they must be tired too.

From where she sat she could see Auntie Bee in

the kitchen. Why did she have to look so much like Mum? It made Teresa's Mum-missing into a real ache.

Bobby Sox rolled onto his back and almost smiled as Teresa inspected his white socks and the funny white splotch on his nose. She dozed a little, but it was an odd sort of sleep. She was always aware of the cat's purring and the little nudges he gave her whenever she stopped patting him. The purring was all mixed up with things Jan and Robert had said.

When she got up about an hour later, Auntie Bee had collected an assortment of empty spools, jar lids and small matchboxes for her on a tray. She'd also brought out a large tin button box.

"I don't know much about kids," she said, "not having any of my own. But I remember I used to make furniture for my dolls' house from bits and pieces like these."

"Oh, thank you!" said Teresa, and she meant it.

Auntie Bee helped her carry it all up to her room and left her on her own. By the time Tom got home, Tape and Curly had settled into the log house as though they'd lived there all their lives. The spools and lids had become tables and chairs. The buttons were tiny footstools, a kitchen sink and pictures for the walls. Teresa had even found an enormous brass belt buckle that made an excellent bathtub.

When Tom came into the room and tossed a shopping bag of new clothes onto his bed, he didn't comment on the furniture in the log house. With his shoes still on, he flopped onto his neatly ironed bedspread.

"There's nothing to do around here," he said. "That TV downstairs is useless. They only get two channels."

When Teresa didn't answer, Tom rolled onto his side and watched as she set up matchbox beds for Tape and Curly in the log house loft.

"What are you doing with those weird dolls, Twig?"

"Their names are Tape and Curly, and they're not weird," said Teresa.

Tom grunted in response.

"Do you see where their beds are, Tom? They're going to sleep in the loft, just like we do at home."

"Wish we were at home now," said Tom, rolling onto his back again and closing his eyes.

Teresa looked at him. He was almost a teenager — surely he wasn't bothered about new things like being away from home! Going off to Max's farm and to a new school would be an adventure for a boy his age. He'd probably even think getting a new leg was a kind of adventure.

"Today they started to make my leg, Tom. It's called a prosthesis."

"Sounds like some kind of dinosaur," Tom mumbled.

"Well, it's not," said Teresa. "And Robert, the man who is making it, is called a prosthetist."

"Like an artist or a dentist?" Tom asked. His eyes were still shut, and his voice sounded kind of dull, but at least he was answering her.

"Don't be silly, Tom," said Teresa.

Tom opened one eye and looked at her. He rolled smoothly off the bed onto the floor and lay still for a moment, long, gangly limbs askew. Then he got up on all fours, stretched like Bobby Sox the cat and crawled over to the house. He reached in and picked up Tape.

"This one's obviously Tape. I see he got mended," he said, sitting back on his haunches.

Teresa watched with amazement as Tom marched him down the log house stairs. Was Tom planning to do something awful like throw Tape out the window?

"Let's make them mountain climb," Tom suggested.

Teresa relaxed a little and picked up Curly. Tape led and Curly followed right up to the top of the bedroom curtains. Tom whistled marching tunes to encourage them on their climb.

"Hand Curly up to me, Twig," Tom suggested when Curly had climbed as high as Teresa could reach.

Tom balanced on the bedstead as Tape and Curly traversed their mountain peak. Then Teresa held out a curtain and they slid all the way down the mountain onto the bed.

After dinner they had one final late-night adventure. Teresa watched as her brother instructed Tape how to ride a hairbrush ATV.

"Tom, let's say he's learning to drive a horse and wagon instead of an ATV, okay?"

"Oh. Right," said Tom. "Tape wouldn't want anymore mending today, would he."

With Tom as his teacher, Tape drove the horse and wagon up and down, up and down, over the lumps and bumps of the yellow-and-white bedspread until it was time to turn out the light.

5.

To the Aquarium

Breakfast was later and more relaxed on Saturday morning. Teresa was relieved that she didn't have to go to the hospital. She wasn't changing her mind about her new leg. She wasn't going to back out now. But there was so much that was new, so much to get used to. She was glad that at least for the weekend she didn't have to think about it.

Auntie Bee and Uncle Edward were free too.

"This will be your only weekend with us, Tom," Uncle Edward said as he caught two pieces of flying toast from an over-exuberant toaster. "Is there anywhere special you'd like to go?"

"When I was here last time," said Tom, accepting one of the pieces, "Dad took me to the Vancouver Aquarium. It was awesome."

Teresa sat up, all ears. "Oh yes, could we go there? They've got a new baby beluga! People at the hospital were talking about it yesterday."

Auntie Bee frowned. "I heard about that baby beluga. It's drawing crowds. We'd probably have to stand in line for ages."

"I don't mind standing in line," said Tom.

But Auntie Bee had caught Uncle Edward's eye. Teresa watched as she raised an eyebrow and glanced in Teresa's direction. She knew what Auntie Bee was fussed about. It was always like this with people she didn't know well. Maybe if she hadn't spoken up and drawn attention to herself … but it was too late now.

Tom had seen the look too. "If you think Twig will find a lineup hard," said Tom, "you don't have to worry. She won't. She's used to that sort of thing. You should see her at my hockey games. They're really crowded and she stands for hours."

Teresa held back a giggle and didn't even mind that he was talking as if she wasn't there. The few people who attended Tom's games weren't what she'd have called a crowd, but his words had worked. Auntie Bee rose from her chair and busied herself putting together a picnic to eat in Stanley Park near the aquarium.

"Let's bring Tape and Curly," Teresa suggested when she and Tom were in their room, making their beds and collecting sweaters.

"Bring the weird dolls?" said Tom. "If you insist."

He scooped up the doll people from their match-box beds, tossed Curly to her and put Tape in his jeans' pocket.

The lineups were long, but there was so much to look at that Teresa didn't mind a bit. Two girls in front of her were playing hand games. They clapped and hopped and slapped their knees, laughing hysterically as the pace became faster and faster.

A dad behind them was trying to control his four sons. The two youngest were twins. They raced around and around their father's legs, ignoring his requests to calm down. The eldest boy and the twins had the whitest blonde hair Teresa had ever seen. The other brother had dark hair. He was about her age and he was staring at her. She stared back.

"What happened to your leg?" he asked.

Auntie Bee and the boy's mum looked startled, but Teresa was used to this sort of question from other kids.

"Lost it in an accident when I was three," she said.

He nodded. "Are you going to get a new one?"

"Yes, I am." It felt good to say it.

"Are you going to see the baby beluga?" the boy asked.

"Hope so," said Teresa.

Somewhere off to the left, a bird was making deep croaky calls.

"Peacocks," said Uncle Edward. "Look! Over there!"

Teresa stared in amazement as one of the enormous, colorful birds spread his fan-shaped tail. He was beautiful.

Tom didn't bother to look. He had other things on his mind. "When I was here last time," he announced to everyone, "I liked the alligators the best." He leaned towards Teresa, closer and closer, until she had to tip backwards, almost losing her balance. He showed his teeth and snapped his mouth open and shut, open and shut, trying to look ferocious. The twins laughed out loud. Teresa didn't. She hoped he'd bite his tongue.

"I doubt an alligator looks like that," the dark-haired brother said.

When they'd finally paid their entrance fees, they moved forward slowly with the crowd. Too slowly for Tom. "I'll find out if there's a lineup to see the baby beluga," he said and raced ahead.

Teresa gazed around in wonder. Fish were everywhere. Some weren't real, like the glass wall of fish, but real fish were swimming in an enormous pool at the side of a sweeping stairway.

Tom returned. "There's a huge lineup for the underwater viewing of the baby beluga," he said. "But come with me. The dolphin show is about to begin."

"Lead the way," said Uncle Edward.

Tom led them down low, right next to the pool. He was up to something, holding Tape out in front of him and wearing a fiendish grin that Teresa knew too well and did not like one bit.

The dolphin was fun to watch. He did spins. Was that why they'd called him Spinnaker? He made his final leap right beside them. In the excitement of the performance, she'd forgotten Tom's look. They were in the splash zone, just as he had planned.

Uncle Edward chuckled as water showered down on them, but Auntie Bee looked none too pleased. In silence she got a handkerchief out of her purse.

Teresa hadn't minded the water, but Tape had received more than his fair share.

"Dry him off," said Teresa crossly.

Tom turned to her with a startled expression on his face. "You mean Uncle Edward?" he whispered.

"No, stupid," she said, giggling in spite of herself. "Tape!"

"Oh, him. He got wet, did he? Sorry, Tape." Tom dried him off with the tail of his T-shirt.

Spinnaker waved goodbye with his tail flukes when his performance was over. The damp group moved on. Tom ran ahead again when Teresa and Auntie Bee stopped to watch playful otters circling, diving deep in their pool, then floating on their backs and holding toys.

The lineup for the baby beluga underwater viewing was still long, but Uncle Edward discovered a spot where they could see perfectly without going down below. They were right beside the announcer, who was talking about the baby's birth. The baby looked tiny beside his enormous mother, a little gray shadow swimming along beside her. As they circled around and around the pool, she always stayed on his outside, protecting him from the edge or from the crowds of people.

"Let's go to the Amazon Gallery next," said Tom.

"Okay," said Uncle Edward, "since it's your special day. But Teresa, we'll come back one day and see that baby beluga from down below, all right?"

"I'd like that," said Teresa.

They found the piranhas that Tom had enjoyed on his visit with Dad. A small sign said the hind ends of the red–bellied piranhas turned red when they were angry.

"I wouldn't want to make them mad," said Uncle Edward. "A group of piranhas can devour a large animal and leave just a skeleton in about two minutes."

"Yuck!" said Teresa.

"Look, Tape," said Tom, holding the doll up to the glass. "Awesome, eh?"

Teresa moved away, thankful for the thick, protective glass. She clutched Curly tightly as she read about the electric eels.

"They used to use the eels' power to light up a little tree during the Christmas season," said Auntie

Bee. "I wonder if they still do."

"Come check out the alligators!" said Tom, pluck-ing at Teresa's sleeve.

Teresa peeked between the people in front of the alligator pool. She could see one of them. He was on the shore on the other side of his pool. He seemed to be staring right at her with his bulbous, dark eyes. His teeth showed even with his mouth closed.

"I bet if I tossed Tape over that glass barrier, he'd snap him up in a flash!" said Tom. He stretched out his arm in a pitch position. The alligator raised his head …

"Don't!" said Teresa, dropping a crutch as she reached forward to stop him.

Tom laughed and darted away.

"Edward, you go with Tom," said Auntie Bee, tak-ing control. "Teresa, you come with me. I've something to show you." She led Teresa, who was close to tears, through a gate and into a magical, tropical rain forest. The room had a glass ceiling, and hun-dreds of exotic, colorful butterflies fluttered through the trees, across their path and up towards the blue sky. Teresa's anger at Tom faded away.

"They're beautiful!" she said, supporting herself against a railing at the side of the path and stretching her arms out wide. Curly was still in one of her hands. "Look, Curly!"

She held the doll up high, and a deep blue butter-fly landed on her head!

Auntie Bee laughed. "She looks like she's wearing a large, exotic hat!"

All kinds of butterflies flew around Teresa and Auntie Bee. A few even landed on Teresa's outstretched arms. She'd like to have stayed longer, but Tom and Uncle Edward joined them. They were hungry and ready for lunch.

Their picnic spot in the park behind the aquarium was beautiful too. They sat under tall trees, at the edge of a sloping, grassy field overlooking the busy harbor.

As they ate their sandwiches, they watched enormous freighters going in and out under Lions Gate Bridge, and seaplanes taking off and flying over the bridge.

Tom pretended to feed ants to Tape, claiming he was hungry after his splash-bath and his close encounter with an alligator.

Teresa watched him closely. At times like this he seemed to like Tape. "You wouldn't really have fed him to the alligators, would you, Tom?"

"Come on, Twig. What do you think?"

Teresa reached for a sandwich. She wanted to think he wouldn't have, so she didn't carry the conversation further. She ate two sandwiches, the most she'd eaten since arriving in the city.

The fun carried on even when they got home. Tom suggested Tape and Curly should join the circus. Tape was hired to run the merry-go-round (the lazy Susan on the kitchen table). Curly did a flying trapeze act, swaying by her feet from the light pull-cord high above them.

Teresa rested her chin on her folded arms and watched as Tom made Tape do a double back-flip off the merry-go-round, then ride bareback on a china horse that was probably one of Auntie Bee's treasures.

She'd never had so much fun with Tom before. At home he never had time for her or her games. Would he miss Tape?

"You really like him, don't you," Teresa said. "I bet you'll miss him."

"Miss who?" Tom asked.

"Tape!" said Teresa.

"Tape?" said Tom in surprise. "But he's just a doll, Twig!"

Sunday wasn't as much fun as Saturday. Auntie Bee and Uncle Edward were busy with chores, and Teresa spent most of her day playing with the dolls' house. Tom did join her for a little while, but mostly he was busy with things that had to be done before he went off to Max's farm.

In the evening, Mum called. Since they didn't have a phone in the house, she called from the pay phone on the porch of the General Store. Dad had stayed at home with Janette and baby John. Tom spoke to her first. Then Teresa had a turn.

Her mother sounded distant and distracted. "It's … it's nice to hear your voice, dear."

"You don't sound like you," said Teresa.

"Well I *am* me. I just don't like phones very much. You know that."

"Oh," said Teresa. Then when Mum didn't reply, she carried on. "Mum? Guess what. Uncle Edward made that little model of our log house into a dolls' house for me. It's just perfect! I wish you could see it."

"Oh, the model," said Mum. "I remember when he and Dad made it. How kind of Edward. I hope you said thank-you."

Teresa twisted the phone cord round and round her little leg. "Yes, I did," she whispered. This wasn't at all like having a conversation with Mum at home. She twisted too much cord, and the phone started to slide across the table, threatening to fall to the floor. She untangled herself.

"How are you doing at the hospital, Teresa?"

Teresa wondered where to begin. Should she tell her about the elevator? All the strangers in the crowded waiting room? Jan? Robert sawing off her cast?

"I hope you're answering when they ask you questions. Not being shy."

"I wish you'd come, Mum."

"From what Tom said, it sounds like you're doing just fine."

Teresa thought about her fun times with Tom and about Tape and Curly, now upstairs in their matchbox beds. "Well, sort of okay, I guess," she managed to say in a shaky whisper.

"Good, good. And you'll be home again in no time."

"Auntie Bee gave me two little dolls to go into the log house, Mum. They're very, very old. One is pink, one kind of light brown, and they look like they're …"

"Oh, those dolls. I remember them! Auntie Bee and I used to play with them when we were your age. Fancy her keeping them all these years. Teresa … I have to go. John has an awful cough and Dad may be having trouble with him. You be a good girl, dear, and we'll talk again soon."

Mum was gone. A dial tone buzzed in Teresa's ear, but she huddled close to the phone and went on talking.

"I call them Tape and Curly, Mum," she said. "Tape is called Tape because he fell apart and had to be mended. Jan mended him with a piece of tape. Get it? We're friends, Curly and Tape and I. Jan and I are friends too. And Robert and Betty and Carlos and …" She couldn't remember any more names. "I … love you, Mum. Bye-bye."

When she hung up, she sat silently for a few minutes on the little stool by the hall phone. She could see

Auntie Bee in the kitchen, tidying up. Quick movements, sharp elbows, just like Mum.

That night she lay on her side for a long time, staring at the log house. She'd forgotten to ask about Janette and Clifford. Did they miss her? Was Clifford lying by the door with his head on his paws, watching and waiting for her?

Neighbors across the street had extra bright lights shining tonight, and it made it look like every light in the log house was burning.

She closed her eyes and imagined those lights going out, one by one, as Mum and Dad went to bed. Then Clifford would fall asleep on the doormat. Maybe she could find a little dog-shaped button in Auntie Bee's button box. Then it could lie by the door of this log house.

6.

The New Leg

When she came down for breakfast in the morning,
Auntie Bee had already left for an early meeting.

"We'll drop you at the hospital," Uncle Edward
said. He had a late shift so he and Tom were going to
be running errands together.

"Drop me?" she asked, remembering the sick-
making elevator and the crowded sixth floor corridor.

"One of us will go up with you," Uncle Edward
reassured her.

When they got to the hospital, there was no place
to park, so Uncle Edward said he'd drive round the
block while Tom went in with Teresa.

Tom walked with her to the elevator, but only
stayed for a minute.

"I gotta go, Twig," he said. "You'll be fine going

up, right? Just get off at the sixth floor." Without waiting for an answer, he turned and left.

Teresa's heart pounded. How could he do this to her? Awkwardly, she reached for the dolls in her pockets.

Holding them, she felt less deserted. But as she tried to settle them in her hands, her right crutch slipped from her grip.

"I caught it," said a voice behind her. Carlos caught the crutch before it hit the floor.

"Knock, knock," he said.

"You don't have to knock," said Teresa. "You just push the button."

"I know that, silly, and I'm not talking about the elevator," said Carlos. "I'm just telling you a semi-stupid joke. You looked like you needed distracting."

"But ..." said Teresa.

"You do know about knock-knock jokes, don't you?"

"Of course I do," said Teresa. It hardly seemed the time. "Who's there?"

"Amos."

"Amos who?"

"Amos Quito bit me."

A lady beside them guffawed loudly as Teresa pushed the elevator button for the third time.

"Knock, knock," said Carlos again.

Teresa had other things on her mind. "Not now, Carlos."

"Come on, Teresa."

She frowned at him, but nothing was going to stop him finishing his joke.

"Who's there?" she whispered. Even though all the people waiting for the elevator were staring with deep concentration at the little numbers flashing by on the small screen above the door, she knew they were listening.

"Andy," Carlos answered.

"Andy who?" she whispered back as quietly as she could.

"Andy bit-me-again."

Everyone laughed except Teresa, and the elevator door opened.

They were packed tight. When they stopped at the second floor, Teresa groaned as her stomach got left behind.

"Bend your knee as it slows next time," said a voice from a back corner. "Believe me, it really helps."

At the next floor, she bent … and so did everyone else, even Carlos on his two prostheses. She turned around to see who had made the suggestion and saw Robert. He must have got on in the basement.

"Thanks," she said, and she bent at each floor after that.

At the sixth floor, as the door opened, Curly slipped from her hand. Teresa gasped and immediately Carlos realized what had happened.

"Careful, everyone, careful," he said loudly, holding up his hand. "Doll emergency."

Everyone had to stream around them while she bent down to rescue Curly. Tom would have looked embarrassed and told her to hurry up, but Carlos stood by her, making sure she didn't get stepped on.

Renovations were still in full swing on the sixth floor.

"We could put on our suction feet and walk along the ceiling," Carlos said, surveying the cluttered corridor.

"Like flies?" Teresa asked. She had a vision of herself walking along upside down. "Do you think there is such a thing?"

"If there isn't, there should be. Perhaps I'll invent them," said Carlos as they maneuvered their way along the hall. "I plan to invent a whole bunch of stuff to help people with prostheses," he added in a more serious tone.

Jan greeted them from across the waiting room with one of her ear-to-ear smiles.

"Doesn't she have an amazing smile?" said Carlos. "Do you suppose she has the usual number of teeth or twice as many as the rest of us?"

"That's mean!" said Teresa.

"No. Not mean. I'd never be mean to Jan. She's the best. But you'll be with her a lot today, so you try to count her sparkling white teeth for me, okay?"

He shot down the hall, dodging people like a football player. She watched him until he was on the elevator. She'd had a whole long conversation with him, and she had hardly felt shy.

Betty was standing on her own by the window. She didn't seem to be looking out; she was just staring into space. As Teresa made her way toward Betty, she thought again how close in age she must be to Janette. She tried to imagine Janette here on her own. It must be so much worse when you were little.

"Betty!" she called out to her. "Come on. Let's go and see what the others are doing."

Betty nodded and came quickly over to her. The children had arranged chairs and a few wheelchairs in a circle.

Teresa and Betty sat down in two empty chairs next to a girl who introduced herself as Susan. She looked about Teresa's age. Maybe they could be friends.

"We're finding out where everyone lives," said Susan. "How about you, Betty?"

"I live in the Kootenays," said Betty, "on a ranch."

"I live on a ranch too!" someone on the other side of the circle said.

"Really?" said Betty, her eyes sparkling.

Everyone joined in. Most of the children lived in or near Vancouver. Susan lived only about an hour away, on a farm in the Fraser Valley.

"And where do you come from, Teresa," Susan asked.

"From the Chilcotin," said Teresa. She looked down at Tape and Curly in her hands. "We live in a beautiful log house. When the moon is full, it shines in the windows, and we can almost read by its light."

What was she saying? Was it her own log house she was describing in such vivid detail? Or Tape and Curly's house, the one Uncle Edward had made over for her?

Susan was staring at her new pink runners. "Kind of cute," she said. "What make?"

"Make?" Teresa asked. "I … I don't know."

"Oh," said Susan. "And do you always carry around those dolls?"

"Not always," said Teresa, slipping them back into her pockets.

"Well, I guess they do help to cheer up little Betty," said Susan.

Teresa gave a slight nod, then wished she hadn't. She was fond of Betty and she loved Tape and Curly.

She spent two hours that morning in the schoolroom. It was kind of like going to school in a long-ago, one-room schoolhouse. Children came and went as they squeezed in their school classes between hospital appointments.

The teacher had been in touch with Teresa's

teacher at home, so in most of her subjects she carried on exactly where she'd left off.

Each student had a different timetable. They were all different ages and working at different levels. Or so Teresa thought, until Susan came along.

"Let me see your timetable," she said, whipping it out of Teresa's hand.

"We'll be in the classroom together three days each week," said Susan.

Teresa smiled weakly.

Recess was called "off time."

"Come on, Teresa, I'll show you where we go," said Susan. Teresa followed her outside to a small courtyard.

"Unless it's pouring or freezing, we play out here," she explained. "It's fun. Otherwise, because of all the renovations, it's back to the crowded, boring, old waiting room."

There were swings and slides, tunnels and monkey bars.

Susan had lost a leg because of an illness. Her new leg was a below-the-knee prosthesis.

"I've only had it for a few weeks," she explained, "but I'm doing really well. Watch."

Teresa watched her crawl in and out of a tunnel, walk hand over hand along the monkey bars and slide down the slide. Teresa's new leg would be different. It would have a knee that she'd have to learn to use.

Would she be able to do these things too?

She sat down on a swing, reached into her pockets and clutched Tape and Curly.

"You're not watching!" called Susan.

"Come and swing," said Teresa. "Let's see how high we can go."

She had mixed feelings when Jan arrived after off time to take her to see Robert. But going with Jan to see her new leg for the first time couldn't possibly be as frightening as meeting Susan for the first time! She turned away to hide her grin.

Robert was waiting for her.

"Here it is!" he said, with a flourish.

He had her new leg laid out on a counter and he was grinning with delight or pride and rubbing his hands together. He was like a chef displaying his masterpiece meal, but her leg was not a banquet!

She stared at all the leg pieces and held Tape and Curly out, so they could see better too.

"So many parts!" she said.

"It has four major parts," Robert explained, pointing to the pieces. "The socket, the knee system, the shank, and the foot and ankle system."

"Looks complicated," said Teresa.

"Only at first," said Robert with a shrug. He handed her the socket to examine. "When you get your more permanent socket, it'll be held on by suction. But this first one is kept in place by a belt that you wear around your waist."

"Today we'll only try on the waist part," said Jan.

"Tomorrow," said Robert, "we'll see how it all fits together and how it fits you."

Jan helped her adjust the belt. It was awkward and dug into her. She hoped her little leg would adapt quickly so she could get rid of the waist part.

As she tried to imagine how a suction socket might work, she lost track of what Robert was saying. Perhaps it was something like the suction cups that Carlos was going to invent for walking on ceilings.

The following day Teresa stood on her new leg for the first time. She looked down at her feet and smiled proudly. They matched. She'd brought in her other pink runner and Robert had put it onto her prosthesis.

She held onto parallel bars at first, like ballerinas do in ballet classes.

After a few shaky minutes, she asked, "Can I let go?"

Robert nodded solemnly. It was not as easy as she had expected it would be. Robert and Jan watched her with such serious expressions, she wondered if she was doing something wrong. But all she had done so far was stand there, trying to keep from falling over.

"Beautiful!" said Robert finally.

"Beautiful?" she asked.

"A perfect fit, he means," said Jan. "And you're doing well, Teresa."

Teresa held on to the bars again and tried a few steps. The knee was going to be her main problem.

"Not to worry," said Jan. "It'll get easier, and you're doing well. Really well."

That evening Teresa watched as Tom squeezed his new clothes into his knapsack and one of Uncle Edward's old duffel bags. He'd be off first thing the next morning.

"I walked on the leg today, Tom," she said.

"Did it hurt?"

"No, not really. It just felt extremely heavy."

"Did you feel like a hardened convict, dragging along a ball and chain?"

"No," said Teresa. "I felt like I wanted to run. But there's no way! I could hardly walk. The knee kept trying to collapse on me."

"Really?" said Tom, as he tied the duffel bag closed.

"Yes, really," said Teresa, her eyes on one log house, her thoughts on another. Tom wasn't even listening. She sat back on her bed, her hands in her pockets, hugging Tape in one hand and Curly in the other.

She tried again to get his attention. "Next week I'll probably get to bring my new leg home, Tom.

Home here, I mean, not home to our real house."

"But I'll be gone," said Tom.

"I know," said Teresa. "If I write you a letter and tell you all about the leg, will you write and tell me about the farm and your school?"

"Sure."

"Promise?"

"I can't promise, Twig. It's not as if I'll be hanging around doing nothing, you know." He looked at her. "But I will try to write."

It was still dark when Uncle Edward came in to wake Tom. Sleepily, Teresa sat up to say good-bye.

Tom's back was to her as he picked up his bags. He hadn't turned on the light, but she could see him clearly, silhouetted by the light from the hall.

At the door, he turned. "Take the bull by the horns, Tree," he said. "You can do it, I know you can." Then he was gone.

Had he really said that? Had he really called her Tree? Happily, she snuggled back under the covers. Maybe he really would miss her. Maybe guys just didn't talk about that kind of mushy stuff, at least not to their sisters. Never mind, he'd promised … well, sort of promised, to write to her. And he'd called her Tree. He'd called her Tree for the first time ever.

7.

Bobby Sox

She went back to sleep, but not for long. Dark shadows still filled the room when a strange sound woke her. It was coming from her log house! Were Tape and Curly making those thumps and bumps? But they were just dolls. She lay still, her heart pounding, wishing Tom were still there.

Someone was hurling the furniture around. But a "someone" wouldn't fit in there, she realized, as she became more fully awake.

She tried to force her eyes to see more in the early gray dawn. The noise stopped, and the silence rang in her ears. Had she dreamed the whole thing? But another sound had started. A rumbling, motor sort of sound. She'd better call out to Auntie Bee! No, she'd be brave, like Mrs. Skiffany's lion. She reached for the light, turned it on and laughed out loud.

Bobby Sox, the cat, had climbed up onto the table at the back of the log house and now he had his whole head and his front paws in the living room. The noises she'd heard would have been his paws, batting all the furniture aside. She could see his head through the living room window, or at least his nose and one eye! He stared at her, unblinking.

"You can stay, Bobby Sox," she said, turning out the light and settling down under the covers for the second time that morning. "Just don't disturb Tape and Curly, okay? The loft is theirs."

Teresa sighed. The log house might not have a dog on the doorstep, but a giant cat had taken over most of the ground floor!

She wrote Tom the next day. There was no immediate reply, but it was haying season. He must be extra busy on the farm.

Teresa was busy too. She began working with a physiotherapist whose name was Sharon. She was kind and encouraging, but Teresa wasn't learning to walk well as fast as she'd hoped. The knee joint kept collapsing and throwing her forward, no matter how hard she concentrated. She couldn't count the number of crash landings she'd had.

She wrote Tom again. She wrote to Mum and Dad, too, and to Janette. She didn't hear back from Tom, but Mum and Dad wrote, wishing her well, and Janette drew her a picture of how they would look when they both learned to skate.

Would such a thing ever be possible?

Susan was no help at all. "Some people just have a harder time," she said, when Teresa tried to share her problems.

Carlos was easier to talk to. He even pretended not to notice when Teresa couldn't hold back her tears. "You should have seen me at first," he said. "With two new legs I had twice the trouble!"

But he was a star in Teresa's eyes. She liked the way he swaggered down the hospital halls. Would she ever walk that well?

Each morning she got Curly and Tape up from their matchbox beds and put them in her pockets. It was comforting to have them with her, even if nowadays they sometimes stayed in her pockets all day long.

Teresa's problems seemed to shrink the day Betty pointed out the new girl.

"She's missing an arm *and* a leg," Betty informed her in a whisper. "I heard two nurses talking about it."

"A car accident, I bet," said Susan.

Betty nodded. "She had cuts on her head, too. That's why they shaved off all her hair."

Teresa glanced at the girl's hunched shoulders. Jan was trying to talk to her, but she wasn't responding at all.

"She sure is grumpy, isn't she?" said Susan.

"I think she's sad," said Teresa.

"Aren't we all?" said Susan.

"Maybe we can help her," said Teresa.

"Maybe," said Susan, "but I can't think how."

When Teresa finally wore her new leg home, Auntie Bee and Uncle Edward helped her celebrate. They had pizza, her favorite dinner, and ate it in the living room while they watched a special video.

Bobby Sox couldn't sit on her lap while she was managing her tray of food, but he stayed right by her chair.

"Look at that crazy cat," said Auntie Bee. "He's sniffing every inch of your new leg."

"He's wondering if it's me," said Teresa.

As she unstrapped her new leg that night, Bobby Sox watched her every move.

"I wish Tom was here," Teresa said as she laid the leg on his bed. "I'd like to show it to him."

"Write and tell him about it," said Auntie Bee. "I can give you stamps."

Teresa sighed. "I have stamps," she said. "Mum gave me stamps and addressed envelopes. I've written him three times. He just never answers."

Auntie Bee changed the subject and pointed at the cat. He had his whole head in the log house. "Now look what he's doing! Has he ever done that before?"

Teresa nodded. "Tape and Curly sleep in the loft, and Bobby Sox sleeps like that, with his head in the living room. I think he likes to look out the window and spy on me while I sleep."

"He's making an awful mess of all your things," said Auntie Bee.

"We don't mind," said Teresa.

"We?"

"Tape and Curly and me. We just set it up again each morning."

Bobby Sox found a new place to sleep that night. When Teresa woke in the morning, she discovered him on Tom's bed with his head in the socket of her new leg.

He didn't like it one bit when she removed him. He hissed at her and stalked from the room. Teresa decided he looked a little like Susan.

8.

The Brilliant Idea

Gradually, they learned more about the new girl. Jan explained that she really needed their support. Not only had she lost an arm and a leg in the car crash, but she'd also lost her father and her brother.

Her mum had survived. She was sometimes with the girl in the waiting room, but she had not fared well in the accident either. She was also in a wheelchair, and though she hadn't lost limbs like her daughter, she had several broken bones and casts on both her legs.

Teresa sat down beside the girl one morning. "What's your name?" she asked.

The girl said nothing.

"Would you like to hold one of my dolls?"

The girl didn't speak or even nod, but she slowly put out her hand. Teresa placed Curly in her open palm. The girl closed her fingers tightly around the doll.

"Her name is Curly," said Teresa.

"I'm Louise," said the girl.

"I guess you're going to have a prosthesis just like mine," said Teresa.

Louise looked over at Teresa's leg. Teresa bent her knee back and forth skillfully, thinking again how great it was to see two pink runners instead of just one.

Betty joined them. "You get to have two prostheses, 'cause I guess you get to have an arm like mine, as well. Wow! You'll get to choose patterns for both of them!" Betty paused, looking thoughtful. "I wonder if you'll choose the same pattern for both your arm and your leg."

"My leg is just boring and plain now," said Teresa. "It's what we get at first. But soon I'll be choosing a pattern like Betty did."

Louise tried to return the doll when Jan arrived to take her to see Robert. Teresa stopped her.

"You can keep Curly for today if you like."

Louise smiled and nodded. Jan gave Teresa one of her stunning ear-to-ear smiles.

Teresa watched as Jan wheeled Louise away. How unbearable it must be for her! She would never see her father and her brother again.

Susan had joined them, but she said nothing until

Louise was out of earshot. "You realize, of course, Teresa, that dinky little doll is gone for good."

"No, she's not," said Teresa.

And she was right. Curly went with Louise to visit Robert that morning, but she came back to Teresa at the end of the day.

After that she often went with Louise to her various hospital appointments. But with a shy smile and a whispered thank-you, Louise always brought her back to Teresa at the end of the day.

Summer ended and autumn began.

"Tom started at his new school today," Auntie Bee said one afternoon.

Teresa sighed. "And he still hasn't written to me!"

"Why don't you write him one more letter," said Auntie Bee. "And we'll make him some fudge to send with it."

Yes, Teresa thought. Tom was bound to answer if she sent him fudge!

"We'll make lots," said Auntie Bee, "so there will be enough left over for us. Your Uncle Edward loves fudge so much I have to hide it from him and bring out just one piece at a time."

Making fudge with Auntie Bee was fun. Teresa stirred as Auntie Bee added each ingredient. With each swirl of the chocolaty mixture, Teresa thought about Tom. Why hadn't he written? It wasn't fair. He could at least have sent a short note.

Auntie Bee found a flat box for the candy. Teresa came up with a brilliant idea. She'd include something else, as well. Something extra special. And she'd give Tom one more chance to respond.

Teresa watched closely as Auntie Bee showed her how to cut and wrap the fudge. Then she offered to complete the task on her own while Auntie Bee got on with making dinner.

One by one she wrapped each piece of fudge in waxed paper. One by one she fitted them into the box. Before putting on the lid, she took three pieces out of the box and slipped Tape in.

Should she tell Auntie Bee what she was doing? No. Auntie Bee had given the dolls to her, not to Tom, and she might be hurt or mad if she knew Teresa was giving one of them away. But Teresa felt sure that what she was doing was not wrong. Tom was lonely and Tape would cheer him up.

Auntie Bee mailed the box with its secret stowaway on a Monday. That same day, Jan suggested to some of the children, including Teresa, that it was time to learn to get around the city. They would all go together at first, but when they were used to it, the older children would learn to take buses on their own.

Louise was not able to go with them. She would need several weeks of physio before she'd be ready. She watched dejectedly as the children prepared to depart.

"Louise," said Teresa, "Curly doesn't want to go. She wants to stay with you. Would that be okay?" Louise beamed and nodded.

Teresa did all right on the sidewalks near the hospital, but when they took a bus downtown she hated it. She was right in the middle of the masses of people that she'd only seen from car windows up until now.

If one of those rushing, frowning people knocked her down, the rest of them would probably walk right over her. She held her head high. Her hands went to her pockets in search of Tape and Curly. But Tape was on his way to Tom, and she'd lent Curly to Louise.

Carlos, walking beside her, gave her an encouraging smile. "It's best to keep your hands out of your pockets," he said. "It's easier to balance that way."

Teresa nodded.

"Great Scott!" she heard someone say. "They're all amputees!"

"Yes," Susan mumbled beside her. "Amputees, so what? At least we're polite, not rude like you."

Being polite wasn't exactly one of Susan's strong points!

Back in the waiting room, Carlos saw Louise hand Curly back to Teresa.

"Where's Tape?" he asked.

"Yes, where is he?" one of the others asked.

"He's gone to visit my brother."

Carlos gasped. "You *sent* him?"

Teresa nodded happily. "I sent him to Tom with some fudge."

"Oh, no!" said Carlos. "Teresa, why?"

"I think it was kind of you," said Betty. She gazed at Teresa with an admiring smile and frowned at Carlos. "You're probably just jealous because she didn't give Tape to you!"

"Get real!" said Carlos. "Oh, Teresa, you shouldn't have!"

"What do you mean I shouldn't have?" Teresa glowered at him. "What do you know about it anyway?"

Carlos raised his voice. "Teresa, boys don't ... boys don't ..."

"Boys don't what?" she shouted. "Play with dolls? Well, Tom does!"

"His friends at the school will think he's a wimp!" said Carlos.

"They won't even know! I sent him to Tom at Max's farm, not to his school, Stupid!"

"Well that's something, at least," said Carlos.

Such a ruckus was unusual in the sixth floor waiting room, where everyone spoke in whispers and walked on tiptoes. Heads turned in surprise and Jan, having just left the room to hang up her coat, chose this moment to return.

"Teresa! Carlos! Simmer down! What on earth is going on?"

No one explained, but quiet was restored.

Teresa gave Carlos a final withering look, then turned to listen to Jan.

"You all did well on our excursion," Jan said. "Before you know it, you'll be riding buses on your own."

"Like me," said Susan proudly. "Next time I go home to the farm, I'm going to take the bus all on my own."

"Good for you, Susan," said Jan.

Teresa wished she were brave enough to do something like that. But maybe it didn't matter anyway. She wasn't old enough to have to do it on her own yet, and soon she'd be going home where there were no crowds.

Tom's reply took a long time to come. Teresa began to think the fudge hadn't done the trick. Then, two weeks later, she came home to discover the letter had finally arrived.

"I'll read it aloud," she said, as Auntie Bee put milk and cookies on the table. But when she'd ripped open the envelope and saw Tom's opening words, she read on in silence.

Dear Twig:

You wanted a letter. So here it is. You made a real fool of me. They made me open the package on the school bus because you could smell chocolate even through the wrapping. They laughed so hard when they saw I'd been sent a DOLL, they actually rolled in

*the aisle. It was the worst thing that has ever happened
to me.*

*I flushed Tape down the school toilct. If you'd been
there I would have flushed YOU!*

From Tom

Teresa burst into tears.

"It's not bad news, is it?" Auntie Bee asked.

She shook her head, but she couldn't speak. She
stumbled on the stairs as she bolted to her room. Poor
Tape. He had probably traveled through miles and
miles of underground drainpipes by now. He might
even be far, far out to sea. She hoped his sides would
stay stuck together. If he fell apart he'd sink down,
down, into the depths of the deep, dark ocean and lie
there in pieces like a sunken boat wreck.

She lay on her bed with Curly on the pillow beside her. Because of the way Curly's right arm curved
up to her mouth, it looked as though she was search-
ing for an answer.

"Don't look like that," said Teresa. "We already
know the answer. Tom is mean and he doesn't even
like me. He's dumb, too. He's so stupid he opened
the package on the bus."

Curly said nothing.

She heard Auntie Bee come up the stairs and pause
for a moment by her door. Fortunately, she went away
without knocking. Teresa felt as if she were reliving

her first day in Vancouver, only worse.

She hadn't noticed Bobby Sox behind the log house. He jumped up beside her and curled up close, purring so hard he almost rattled the bed. Teresa patted him absentmindedly and tried to cry quietly so Auntie Bee wouldn't hear.

9.

Misery

At dinnertime, Uncle Edward made Teresa feel worse than ever when he passed her the now almost empty tin of the fudge that had started it all.

"Won't you tell us what's upset you?" he asked.

Frowning at the tin, Teresa shook her head.

"What did Tom say in that letter?" Auntie Bee asked.

Teresa bowed her head and mumbled into her chin. "Nothing."

"It was a letter, Teresa, so he obviously said something," said Auntie Bee. "And it was something that has upset you."

Teresa tried to stop their questions without giving it all away. "It's not the letter," she said. "It's just that everyone expects me to do stuff that I don't want to do." Then she quickly added, "At the hospital, I mean."

They exchanged questioning looks, but they didn't keep at her, like Mum would have done.

Mum would have said, "Teresa, enough is enough. Let's get to the bottom of this."

They were being kind. If she told them what she'd done they'd probably be far more understanding than her own parents would. But she couldn't. She'd know by their tone that they thought she was stupid, just like Carlos did.

She pushed back her chair and stood up.

"I guess I'm just tired," she said, in little more than a whisper. "I think I'll go to bed now."

Auntie Bee and Uncle Edward looked a little surprised.

"Teresa," said Auntie Bee, stopping her in her tracks, "you forgot something."

Had she not excused herself politely enough? Uncle Edward pointed to her place. Curly was still lying on the table next to Teresa's plate. Teresa picked her up and clasped her tightly.

"Thanks," she said.

Her aunt and uncle nodded and wished her good-night.

She wondered if they had noticed Tape's absence. Probably not. Even if they did, they'd just think he was in her pocket or in the log house upstairs.

The last thing Teresa wanted to do the next morning was get up and go to the hospital. But though Auntie Bee and Uncle Edward looked sympathetic when she said she felt sick, they would not let her stay home alone.

It was a horrible day. Rain came down in buckets. On the way to the hospital even Uncle Edward looked grim.

Teresa slipped getting out of the car, soaked her jeans as she hit the pavement and scraped the palms of both her hands. Everyone was kind and helpful, but they simply encouraged her to get quickly out of her wet jeans and into her shorts for physio. No one suggested that she should go home.

None of the physios were in the big room where Teresa did her exercises. Carlos and a few of the other kids were taking advantage of their absence and rolling around the room on the physios' stools.

"Come on, Teresa," said Carlos. "Grab one. It's fun." She frowned at him. Had he forgotten how horrid he'd been to her?

When the physios returned and the other kids were scolded, she was glad. It served them right.

She struggled through her exercises with Sharon. Everything seemed extra hard. Mrs. Skiffany had made her think that getting a new leg would be a breeze. Well, it wasn't. Old Skiffy just didn't know. Teresa frowned when Jan tried to encourage her to eat her lunch. "Teresa, what's bothering you?" she asked, but Teresa pretended she hadn't heard.

Each morning that week was the same. Teresa did the things she was supposed to do, but her heart wasn't in it. Whenever she saw Carlos, she turned away. Under cover of her pocket, she clutched Curly. She couldn't bring herself to lend her to Louise anymore. But whenever her fingertips touched the little doll, she thought of Tape and his horrible ending.

"Why so glum, chum?" Sharon asked after several days. "What's the matter with my star pupil?"

"Nothing's the matter," Teresa replied. "It's just that it's too hard!"

"It is hard," said Sharon. "But we don't do easy things around here. Besides, *hard* has never stopped you before. I thought you liked a challenge."

Teresa set her mouth and tried a little harder. But as one little voice urged her to try, another was saying, I did just fine on my crutches. I don't need this dumb leg.

The schoolroom wasn't any better. She ruined three whole math worksheets by adding when she was supposed to subtract and subtracting when she was supposed to add. And she was smart in math!

One morning she bumped into Robert in the elevator. He stood beside her, smiling and bending his knees at each stop. "Not only does all this bending help the stomach, but it's good training for prosthetic knees," he said.

"Yes," said Teresa without enthusiasm.

They walked along the sixth floor corridor together. It was a little less busy here now. Most of the work was being done one floor up.

"Soon we'll be building your streamlined leg with the suction socket," Robert announced. "I did tell you, didn't I, that you could go ahead anytime now and pick your pattern?"

Teresa nodded. "Yes, you told me."

But she hadn't got around to picking. What difference would the pattern make? Did it really matter whether it was plain, polka dotted or covered with flying purple people eaters?

Teresa saw Robert's look of bewilderment, but didn't realize the depth of his concern. Right after their meeting, he consulted with Jan. That afternoon Jan hailed Teresa in the hall.

"I want to see you in my office," she said.

"But I'm due in the schoolroom."

"Now," said Jan.

Teresa had not even realized Jan had an office. She held back at the door of the closet-sized room. Jan ushered her in and cleared away a pile of books and papers from the one chair.

"Sit," she said.

Teresa sat. Jan perched on the edge of her desk.

"I've felt like a spy these past few weeks, trying to find out what's made you so miserable," she began.

"Sharon is concerned. You're not doing as well as usual in the schoolroom. Robert is beside himself. Now, though, thanks to Carlos, I think I've solved the mystery. Teresa, he told me about you sending Tape to Tom."

Teresa sat bolt upright. "Carlos had no right …"

Jan held up a hand. "Maybe you don't think so," she said. "But even your aunt and uncle dropped by because they were worried about you. They think you're just homesick, but they happened to mention that you'd had a letter from Tom. A letter you wouldn't talk about. I put two and two together."

Teresa crossed her arms. "I'm still working like I'm supposed to!"

Jan stopped her again. "Teresa, you're going through the motions every day. You're following your schedule, but you've lost your spark, your gumption. And your unhappiness is affecting your progress."

Teresa let her hair fall over her face. If she cried, she didn't want Jan to see her tears.

Jan squeezed her shoulder. "What did Tom say in that letter? He wasn't happy about you sending the doll, was he?"

Teresa shook her head. Her voice trembled when the words finally came. "I was just trying to help him."

"Help him?"

"I thought he must be lonely, so I shared."

"That was a kind thing to do. I know how much Tape meant to you."

"Well he sure didn't mean anything to Tom! He flushed him," Teresa said furiously.

"He what?"

"Flushed him. Down the toilet."

"Maybe he just said that."

"No, he did it. I know he did. I know Tom."

Jan sighed. "Teresa, believe it or not, I really, truly sympathize," she said, "because I know how much you must be missing your family, especially your brother."

Teresa bristled. She felt angrier with Tom at that moment than she'd felt in weeks. She wouldn't be in trouble now if he'd just written like he said he would.

"I hate Tom," she said. "I don't miss him one bit!"

"Umm, right," said Jan.

They sat in silence for a few minutes. Then Jan looked at her watch and leapt to her feet.

"Look at the time, Teresa! I've made you late for school and I had an appointment fifteen minutes ago!" Then she added more gently, "We'll talk again soon."

Teresa nodded and got up. She might talk with Jan again. She'd think about it.

She saw Louise in the hall on the way to the schoolroom, and she saw her again at off time. Betty was talking to her. She wanted to go over to them. She wanted to share Curly with Louise again. But she couldn't bring herself to move from the swing where she was sitting. Instead, she swung back and forth, dragging the toes of her pink runners through the dirt.

Susan was on the swing next to her, going on and on about the upcoming long weekend. Teresa was only half listening. She was busy thinking about ways she could tell Tom off. Usually it was the other way around. But now it was her turn. Should she phone him? But phones were so unfriendly — not that she wanted to be friendly with Tom.

"We're getting out early on Friday, you know," Susan said. "I'll be leaving right after lunch. I'm going to take the bus to Langley all by myself. I've taken it with my parents lots of times, but this time I'm taking it on my own. The driver is going to let me off right at my gate."

Teresa's ears perked up. "Is that where you live? In Langley?"

"Well, near Langley," said Susan.

"Do you know Max Solesky?" Teresa asked.

"Who?"

"Max Solesky. He's my dad's friend and he lives in Langley too. That's where my brother Tom is staying."

"I don't think I know him."

"Oh," said Teresa.

"Where's your brother going to school?" Susan asked.

Teresa tried to remember. "It's a name like Freeman or Foreman. It's a high school, a secondary school.

A school where they play a lot of hockey."

"Freedman Secondary. That's just across the road from our place!" said Susan.

Everyone was given a note that afternoon about the half day off. When she got home after school, Teresa took her note from her pocket. She was about to hand it to Auntie Bee when she changed her mind.

She'd curl up with Bobby Sox in the basket chair and have a little think first.

10.

The Long Weekend

On Friday, Teresa waited until off time to talk to Susan.

"By the way," she began in the coolest tone she could muster, "I'm going to Langley too."

"You are?" Susan looked surprised. "You mean you're going out to see your brother?"

"Yes," said Teresa. "I'm meeting him at his school. It's all arranged." A tight knot formed in her innards. She hated lying.

"Are you going on the bus?"

Teresa nodded.

"How are you getting to the bus depot?" Susan asked.

Teresa's heart sank. She hadn't thought about that detail. But Susan spoke again, before she could answer.

"Mum and Dad gave me money for a taxi. You

can share with me if you want to."

"That would be great," said Teresa.

But she had not counted on how closely supervised they would be. Their teacher from the schoolroom came to the front door to see Susan on her way.

"Teresa," she said, "what are you doing here?"

"I'm going with Susan," Teresa said, her heart thumping. "I'm going to Langley too, to see my brother." It wasn't exactly a lie.

The teacher looked concerned, but the taxi driver had the door open, waiting.

"No one told me there'd be two of you," she said.

"Lady, if these kids are going to make the one forty-five bus, I've got to move it," said the taxi driver.

"Well, you are a dependable girl," the teacher said to Teresa. "Someone must have forgotten to tell me."

Teresa smiled at her, but the knot inside her grew tighter than ever.

"Don't worry," the taxi driver said. "I've done this loads of times. I'll see they get their tickets and get into the right line."

As the taxi moved off, Teresa's heart beat all the way up into her head. Why was she doing this? She must be crazy. But she had to see Tom, she reminded herself. It was an important mission, and she only felt like this because it was way scarier than she'd expected. She thought it would be just like taking the bus downtown with Jan and the other kids. She hadn't counted on taxis and bus depots.

Teresa looked out the back window of the taxi to make sure no one was following. No one was. Now that she was sitting, she reached into her pocket for Curly, but Curly wasn't there. That morning in the waiting room, for the first time in ages, she'd lent Curly to Louise again. And she'd forgotten to get her back.

She took big breaths. She'd manage. She had to. The worst was surely over. And it wasn't such a terrible thing she was doing. At least, not if she could get out there, see Tom and get back before the Mullans missed her. How much time did she have? She hadn't worked that out, either.

The woman at the ticket booth looked at Susan and raised an eyebrow. "I recognize you," she said. "But who is your friend?"

Teresa's heart stopped, but only for a second.

"She's Teresa," Susan said. "She's going to Langley too. To see her brother."

Teresa nodded. This time Susan's bossiness was okay. She handed the woman a ten-dollar bill. It was all the money she had in the whole wide world.

"That's not quite enough for a return ticket," said the woman.

Teresa thought fast. "I don't want a return ticket. I only want one way."

"I didn't know that," said Susan. "How are you

getting back then?"

"My … um … my uncle is coming out later to-night to get me."

"Tonight? I thought you were staying for the week-end?"

"I mean, ah, tomorrow," said Teresa.

"Weird," said Susan. "Since it's a long weekend you'd think they'd let you stay till Monday."

"Pick up your change, dear, and move along," said the ticket lady. "People are waiting behind you."

"Come on, Teresa," said Susan. "The taxi man is waiting to show us the right line."

Teresa followed them. If she didn't have enough money, how was she going to get back? Tom was the stingiest person she knew. But she'd make him give her the money. After all, it was his fault that she had to make this trip.

"How long does the bus take?" she asked Susan when they were settled in their big, comfortable seats.

"Not long. Just an hour," said Susan. "I could go back and forth every day, but my mother felt it would be less tiring for me if I stayed in the city. We have friends right near the hospital."

The rain that had continued on all week turned to snow as they crossed the Port Mann Bridge. Teresa stared out the window at the muddy Fraser River. The knot inside her was getting worse instead of better.

"We'll be there in just a few minutes, girls," the driver called back to them as they turned off the highway. "Gather your things. You have to be quick. This is an unscheduled stop I'm making for you!"

A man across the aisle handed down Susan's suitcase from the shelf above them. Teresa had been hugging one small knapsack on her lap all the way. She twisted sideways in the seat to get it onto her back. She should have put in PJs and a toothbrush.

She tried to walk erect as they scrambled from the bus. The driver waved. The doors closed and the bus shot off, swirling up the gathering snow behind it. The wind was howling now.

Susan pointed across the highway at a long, low building. "That's the school, right there." She glanced down the farm road beside them and waved. "Here comes my mum ... she's walking out to meet me."

"Great!" said Teresa, trying to make her voice sound normal and cheerful. "I'd better get over there. Tom will be waiting. I'll see you Tuesday."

Susan's mother was getting closer. Teresa waited for a farm truck to pass on the highway. It blew stinging snow into her face. Then, head held high, she crossed.

When she was safely on the other side, she turned to wave to Susan. It was easier to face her than it was to face the building before her. The school was forbidding. This whole exercise was forbidding. She considered hiding behind a tree and waiting until the bus came back. It probably would come back this way. But she didn't have enough money for the ticket.

As she stood freezing on the school driveway, a bell rang and two yellow school buses turned off the highway and came towards her. She slipped and slid her way to the sidewalk, stepping through the thin ice of a deep puddle on the way. She looked down at her feet. Her pink runners were soaked.

No turning back now. She marched forward and pushed open the heavy front door.

The noise almost knocked her over backwards. There were hundreds of kids. How on earth had she ever expected to find Tom? The office was right beside her. It had a glass front, and a woman with a kind face was looking her way. She was talking to a tall man.

Teresa opened the office door. "I have to see Tom," she said.

The woman with the kind face stopped talking in mid-sentence.

The man looked down at Teresa. "Tom?"

"Yes, my brother," said Teresa, standing as tall as she could. He towered over her. The snow on her face was melting. Drip after drip fell from the tip of her nose.

"We'll need a last name," said the woman in a gentle voice.

"Oh, sorry," said Teresa. "Tom Joseph."

"Ah, that Tom," said the man. He looked more pleasant now. "He's in my homeroom. I'll see if he's still here. You may be too late."

Too late? But before she could panic, Teresa heard Tom's voice.

"Twig?"

She swung around. Tom stood in the doorway with a bewildered expression on his face.

"What are you doing here? Has something bad happened?"

She kept her expression as blank as she could. She couldn't turn into a crybaby now. "I have to talk to you."

Tom looked baffled. His mouth opened and shut, opened and shut again, as if he wanted to say something, but not in front of the two teachers. She didn't want to either.

"Look," said the woman, "I think you two had better use my office so you can talk in private."

Teresa swallowed, nodded and followed her into a back room.

"Twig, you're walking without your crutches!" Tom said from behind her. "That's fantastic!" His words were kind enough, but his voice sounded false and forced.

He turned to the woman who had been holding the door. "Thank you, Mrs. Reid."

Mrs. Reid left and the door closed softly. They

were alone. Tom sank down onto a straight-backed chair by the door.

Teresa looked around her, stalling for time as she tried to decide what to do next. When she'd imagined this encounter, she'd never got this far! She noticed a plaque on the desk. *Principal*, it said. Mrs. Reid was Tom's principal. She gave Tom what she hoped was a haughty look and moved behind the desk. Her legs felt wobbly — both of them. She rested her arms on the desk for support and frowned across at her brother.

"I don't get this," said Tom. "Tell me why you're here. And why you're so mad."

"As if you didn't know, Tom." But she was beginning to wonder herself. Why had this trip seemed so important? She mustn't cry. She swiveled Mrs. Reid's chair around to face the window. Outside, kids were playing in the schoolyard as if everything were normal.

"How did you get here? Auntie Bee and Uncle Edward do know, don't they?"

Teresa swung back around from the window. "No, they don't! No one knows. And if I get in trouble it will be all your fault. You forced me to come."

"Me?"

"Shut up, Tom! Just shut up!"

"Teresa!"

"You never wrote … till that horrible letter. And you suspected me, Tom. You are so horrible. So totally, totally, horrible."

"I don't get it," Tom said finally, shaking his head and frowning. "How do you mean, I *suspected* you?"

"You know what I mean. You thought I sent Tape just to embarrass you and I did not!"

There. It was done. She sank lower in the principal's chair, laid her head on the principal's desk and let the tears come.

When she finally looked up, she saw that he was crying too. She'd never seen Tom cry. He was sitting bolt upright on the straight chair. The tears rolled down his cheeks, not in flowing rivers like hers, but one by one. In two processions they rolled down his cheeks, around the curve of his chin and disappeared under the collar of his T-shirt. He didn't even try to wipe them away.

"I know you won't believe me, but I was sorry the minute I sent you that letter. I should have called you. I don't know whether I can explain, Twig, but please let me try?"

Teresa nodded.

"It was so awful when I first came here," said Tom.

"You mean at the farm?"

"No, no. It was fine there. Max is cool. The summer was just plain busy. That's why I didn't write then." When Teresa scowled at him, he continued, "I know, I know, I could have written at night or phoned or something."

"Then why didn't you? It was awful for me too, Tom."

"Was it? Yes … I guess I knew that. That was why I kind of … well, got into playing with Tape and Curly with you in the first place. And because I was bored."

Teresa's heart sank to an all-time low. "You didn't really want to?"

"Later I did. Later on it got fun."

"But you flushed Tape."

Tom looked down at the knapsack on his knee and zipped the front zipper open, then closed, then open again.

Teresa watched, wide-eyed. "Is he in there?" she asked, her hopes rising.

Tom shook his head. "I'd only just started to make friends, and then they saw Tape and I knew I was finished."

"But why did you take my package on the bus in the first place?"

"The mail guy came by right as I was about to get on the bus and handed it to me. Plunk. Right into my hands instead of into the mailbox at the gate."

"So you opened it," said Teresa quietly.

"Yeah. 'He plays with dolls,' they said, and, 'Oh, look, it's wearing diapers. A baby dolly for little Tommy.' They tortured me."

"So you tortured Tape," said Teresa bluntly. "You flushed him,"

"I didn't know what else to do," said Tom desperately. "I wanted to show them what I thought of dolls.

I did it in front of them. Right away I wished I hadn't."

"I bet you didn't!"

"I did, honestly. I went back to the washroom later to see if maybe he hadn't gone down. But he had. It was too late."

There was a knock at the door. Another stranger.

"Max!" said Tom. "This is Teresa, my sister."

Like Mrs. Reid, the man at the door looked kind. But now the clock on the wall said three-thirty. Auntie Bee would be at the hospital, waiting for her at the door. How had she ever thought she'd make it back in time?

"Teresa! Nice to meet you, finally," said Max and held out his hand.

"Max," said Tom, "do you think we could call Auntie Bee on the office phone and let her know Teresa got here safely? And could we maybe keep her for the weekend?"

11.

Determination

Afterwards, Teresa wondered how she'd ever found the words to tell Auntie Bee how sorry she was.

"You gave me the scare of my life, Teresa," Auntie Bee had said.

Teresa liked her aunt. She hadn't wanted to scare her. But by the time Tom and Teresa had contacted her, Teresa's friends at the hospital had been in an awful spin.

Miraculously, despite the kerfuffle, Teresa had been allowed to stay. And even more miraculously, Tom had been nice to her all weekend long.

On Saturday, when Tom was busy with weekend chores, Max drove Teresa around the farm in an old truck, just like Dad's. He was a little bit like Dad, only he talked more.

"We were buddies, your old man and I," he told Teresa. "We got into all kinds of mischief together." He looked at her with a twinkle in his eye. "Like you taking that bus ride, we went places together. We rode empty rail cars across the country; we hitched in the back of trucks. We were rolling stones. I'm surprised we ever settled down."

The early snowfall continued all weekend. Learning to walk on the snow and ice with her new leg was a real challenge for Teresa. It was great, though, because Max gave her lots of encouragement, and Tom even followed his example and cheered her on.

The countryside was beautiful. The cattle wore snow coats on top of their winter fur. Some stood so still that they looked like statues until they blew white puffs of steam from their nostrils.

Teresa liked Max's cows. She liked letting them lick her fingers with their sandpaper tongues. She liked feeding them handfuls of hay when Tom was busy setting up for milking.

It wasn't quite so much fun when Tom handed her a shovel and she had to help him muck out the stalls, but she did it.

She and Tom didn't share a room like at the Mullans, but they spent a lot of time, just the two of them, on their own.

On Sunday night, Teresa brought up the subject of Tape one last time.

"Where do you think he is now?" she asked.

"He's in Nanaimo," Tom said.

"Where's that?" Teresa asked.

"It's on Vancouver Island," said Tom. "It's a great place. He's living with a really nice couple, the O'Rourkes. They have tons of grandchildren who visit them all the time."

His face was so serious, Teresa almost believed him. "Tom, that's impossible. How would you have heard that he was there?"

"I heard," Tom replied knowingly, "from a bird."

Teresa burst out laughing. "That's silly, Tom!"

Her brother ignored her. "To make a long story short," he said, "Tape traveled down sewer pipes and ended up in the sea. A girl your age, Emily, was on her dad's fishboat and saw him. She scooped him up in a fishnet. He had all kinds of adventures on that fish-boat, but then he fell overboard in a storm. He's a great swimmer, though, or at least a great floater. So he bobbed along. A long, long way along, until he flowed with the incoming tide into a safe protected lagoon in Nanaimo."

Teresa sighed. "Tape always did love adventures, didn't he?"

"He did indeed," said Tom.

Tom didn't have a holiday on Monday. But before he left for school, Teresa had breakfast with him while Max was busy in the barn.

"Tree," he said, "I meant what I said about your leg. You really are doing well."

"Thanks," said Teresa.

"So now we let bygones be bygones?" Tom asked.

"Depends what that means …" said Teresa.

"Bygones are things that happened a long time ago. And it sort of means we'll forget about those things."

"I'll try to forget the bad bygones," said Teresa, "but I won't forget the good ones."

"I won't forget the good ones either," said Tom.

Max took Teresa to the bus depot in Langley to catch the bus back to Vancouver. The bus picked up Susan, who was waiting by her farm gate.

"You stayed for the whole weekend after all! You should have phoned me. You could have come over!"

"We were pretty busy," said Teresa.

She didn't tell Susan the whole story, but she talked about Tom a little and about Max's farm. The trip back to town was much more fun. She and Susan laughed together as they watched a two-year-old who was determined to turn somersaults in the aisle. And they whispered and giggled together when they saw a couple of teenagers trying to kiss without being noticed. Sometimes Susan was an okay friend.

When they arrived in the city, even the crowded bus station didn't seem so bad. The Mullans were there to meet her. Susan's family friends were there to meet her, too.

On the way home, Auntie Bee and Uncle Edward asked Teresa about Tom's school and Max's farm. After dinner, when the "asking permission" subject came up, as it was bound to, they were kind and understanding.

"You will tell us next time you feel you have to see that brother of yours, won't you?" said Uncle Edward.

She could see the concern on both their faces. "Yes, I will," she promised. Her parents would not have let her off half as easily.

She missed her parents. Phone calls were hopeless, letters not much better. She wanted to see them and show them how well she was doing. She crossed her fingers. Hopefully she'd be home by Christmas.

It was December. The snow in the Chilcotin would be deep now. The little lake behind their log cabin would be frozen. During the holidays, they were going to make a rink. She'd told Tom she'd get it started. She was bound and determined that she would be home before him.

12.

Skating Lessons

"Here's Curly," said Louise on Tuesday. "You forgot to take her with you, so I looked after her for you."

"Thanks, Louise," said Teresa, "but I think you should keep her now."

Louise shook her head. "No. You're going home soon, and Curly wants to go with you. She wants to see your log house, the big one up in the Chilcotin that you told me about. Not the one she's lived in here."

Louise was out of her wheelchair now and walking on her first prosthesis, but she was still living in the hospital.

"Tell you what," said Teresa. "You keep her till I leave, okay?"

"I'd like that," said Louise.

Jan and Sharon and Robert agreed that Teresa

would only be allowed to go home when she caught up with the time she had lost. She had not made as much progress in recent weeks as she should have. Teresa worked harder than she'd ever worked before.

She learned to climb the sample steps in the physio room. She climbed the stairs to the second and even the third floors of the hospital every day. She'd never liked the elevator anyway!

She rode the standing bike each day for as long as she was allowed. Outside, she mastered slippery, wet winter sidewalks, icy ramps and busy streets. She wished she'd learned that lesson before her trip to Langley in the snow! She fell much less often now.

"Have you decided on the pattern for your new leg yet?" Robert asked her.

"I have," said Teresa. "I want the hockey pattern."

"Are you sure, Teresa?" Robert asked. "Isn't that a boy pattern?"

"Girls play hockey too," said Teresa. The pattern had all the crests of the NHL teams scattered on a royal blue background.

It was easier to think winter and hockey after the trip to Langley. It didn't snow much in Vancouver, but you could still tell that winter had come.

When the new leg was ready, Robert summoned Teresa, Jan and Sharon to his room.

"Sit on the examining table, Teresa," he said.

Teresa nodded and sat. Robert left the room and Jan and Sharon stood on either side of her. There was an air of excitement in the room.

Robert burst back through the side door. "Ta daaaaa!" he said, carrying the leg high.

"This feels special," said Teresa. "I feel as though I'm receiving a reward."

"You are receiving a reward," Jan said, squeezing her shoulder.

"That's right," said Robert. "You only get a suction socket and a pattern when you've proved yourself."

Teresa giggled. It was just as she had imagined it would be with her first new leg.

When she had put it on, Jan transferred her sock and pink runner from the old leg to the new, and Teresa stood up. They all watched.

"Well, how is it?" Robert asked.

"It feels different, but it's great to get rid of that awful belt around my waist. It's really comfortable!"

She paraded around the small room like a model presenting a new dress.

"That is quite the pattern, Teresa," said Sharon, admiring the hockey crests. "I take it you plan to learn to skate?"

"Yes, I do," said Teresa.

"Then I think we'd better have a lesson together tomorrow, because Jan tells me there's a good chance you'll be going home next week."

Teresa beamed. "I'd … I'd love that! It would be perfect!" She'd surprise Tom! She'd surprise every-one at home!

She bumped into Carlos in the hall.

"You're walking so well," he said. "Must be the cool pattern!"

She stiffened, ready for a quarrel. Was he teasing? Perhaps, but his smile was kind. She smiled back.

"Thanks, Carlos," she said.

The Mullans were almost as excited as she was when she came home wearing the new leg. She told them about the skating lesson she was going to have with Sharon.

"Under these exciting new circumstances," said Uncle Edward, "I think we'd better give you an early Christmas present. You won't be with us on the big day. Let's go shopping for skates right now. The stores are open late."

Sharon took her to an inside rink, a first for Teresa. She'd never seen one before. They went at a quiet time of day. "So we won't be slamming into too many peo-ple," Sharon explained.

It was colder inside than outside. With Sharon helping her, Teresa got her skates on first. Then she rose cautiously to her feet and grinned at Sharon.

"Walk around a bit if you like while I'm getting

mine on," said Sharon. "But don't go on the ice till I'm ready."

Teresa nodded and walked carefully over to the open gate. At the Mullans', she'd practiced walking a little wearing her guards. She watched a woman having a skating lesson.

The instructor's voice echoed up to the high ceiling.

"Higher! Higher! Gently now. Come on! Watch that left arm!"

He didn't seem too happy with his student's progress, but Teresa thought she was magical. She floated across the ice as if it took no effort at all, just the way Teresa sometimes did in her dreams. She watched, entranced, as the skater glided forwards and backwards. She did great leaps into the air and came down without falling.

Sharon came up behind her. "Teresa, this is going to be fun, but it's not going to be like that," she warned, pointing to the skater. "She's a professional. Few of us ever learn to make those moves."

"I know that," said Teresa.

She took a deep breath, took hold of the support that Sharon held ready and stepped onto the ice. She knew she didn't look like the figure skater, but in her heart she felt just like her! She held on tight, pushed with her real leg and glided forward on her appropriately decorated prosthesis.

Skating without the support was another story. She was on her bottom more than she was on her feet, and it wasn't easy getting up from the slippery ice.

"Keep the new leg directly under your body," Sharon advised, taking her arm and hauling her to her feet. "It'll come, Teresa. It'll come."

Teresa's gliding was far from graceful that first day. But despite a bruised bottom and a scraped chin, she loved every minute of it.

On the weekend, the Mullans took her back to the rink. They went early in the morning to get there before the crowds.

While it was quiet, Teresa used Uncle Edward's hockey stick as a support. She felt like a real hockey player! When the rink became crowded, she held her aunt's and uncle's hands and skated between them. They circled the rink, round and round, in time with the wonderful music. Teresa felt like she was flying.

She and Sharon squeezed in two more lessons the following week. Gradually, Teresa was learning to glide.

"You'll find you glide much farther on your real leg than you do on your prosthesis," Sharon explained.

It was an odd sort of movement. One long glide, one short one. One long glide, one short one. One of the kids at the hospital had described it to Teresa as a herky-jerky sort of stride, and that was exactly what it was like.

She certainly wasn't ready for the Olympics … but she'd made a start.

Sharon treated Teresa to a hamburger after their final lesson. Then they had a drive around Stanley Park.

"Just so you can see the sea one more time, and you won't forget how gorgeous it is," said Sharon.

She pointed to Lost Lagoon. Ducks and geese were walking on a thin layer of ice near the edge, but it was a long way from being thick enough to skate on.

"On the rare occasion it freezes over," she said. "Then we skate outside. That's a real treat for us!"

"We can only skate outside at home," said Teresa. "I loved the inside rink. You don't get so cold!"

The night before she left for home, Tom called to wish her a safe journey. It was his second call. Maybe he wasn't managing letters, but he was doing his best to keep in touch.

"You'll trick that flight attendant for sure," he said.

"I don't care if I don't," said Teresa, "as long as she gives me the window seat this time!"

"Don't forget to get our rink ready," Tom reminded her. "We'll find some old skates, and I'll teach you to skate."

Teresa gloated. Teach? She'd show him moves he'd never seen before. Well, maybe not … but she'd sure surprise him. She'd bought him a hockey puck for Christmas. It was already packed. Last winter he'd used an old cat food tin filled with water and frozen solid.

"Teresa? Are you there?" Tom asked. "This is a telephone; I can't see you nodding or shaking your head. Which are you doing?"

"I'm nodding my head," said Teresa happily. "I'll have the rink all frozen and ready. Don't you worry."

When she got off the phone, she scooped up Bobby Sox and danced around the living room. He squirmed in her arms.

"Kind of herky-jerky, eh, Bobby Sox? But we don't care, do we? It's fun, and that's the main thing!"

13.

Leaving the Log House

On Teresa's last visit to the hospital, both Uncle Edward and Auntie Bee came with her. They put her suitcase in the trunk and the log house beside her on the backseat. They would be going straight on to the airport after the hospital.

Teresa studied the backs of their heads. Next time she came to Vancouver, Auntie Bee would not have to wear her red hat to be recognized. And Uncle Edward? Well, she'd know him anywhere! She smiled, remembering the first time she'd seen him, or at least the top of his head, from her window.

"We forgot something," said Uncle Edward as soon as the house was out of sight.

"Oh no!" said Auntie Bee. "What?"

"I never took Teresa back to see the baby beluga

from the underwater viewing area. I promised I would!"

"I'll be back," said Teresa.

"I'm glad you will be," said Uncle Edward. "I'm going to miss you."

"Me too," said Auntie Bee, turning to Teresa in the backseat. "We'll keep your room ready for you."

Teresa grinned. She wasn't going to mind coming back for her regular checkups. She'd look forward to sleeping in her special yellow room again.

But now she could hardly wait to see her family. She kept imagining her homecoming, her return to her log house. Would Janette have grown? Would baby John even know who she was? And Clifford ... would he sniff the new leg all over like Bobby Sox had?

She ran her hand across the roof of the log house beside her and dusted off the front windows with a fingertip. "Can I take the log house in to show the other kids?" she asked as they drew into a parking spot at the hospital.

"I don't see why not," said Uncle Edward.

He lifted it out and carried it for her. He'd made a handle on the roof to make carrying easier.

Today she would be saying goodbye to all her hospital friends as well as to the Mullans. Some of them she might never see again; their visits to the hospital might not coincide with hers.

Everything was familiar to her now. The big waiting room no longer seemed bleak or scary. But as she looked around at the wide-eyed waiting patients, she could see that some, especially the younger ones, were feeling just as insecure as she had at first.

Her special friends, the ones she had got to know well, were busily occupied this morning. They were gathered in a tight cluster. She could hear their quiet laughter. Jan was with them.

"What's everybody doing?" she asked.

"Jan gave us pipe cleaners. We're making pipe cleaner people," Betty explained. She held one up for Teresa to see.

Louise's thin face lit up when she spied the log house in Uncle Edward's arms. "Oh, Teresa, is that Curly's house? The log house you told me about that's just like yours?"

Teresa nodded.

The circle of children opened and reformed around Uncle Edward and the house.

"This is my uncle," said Teresa. "He and my father made the house."

Uncle Edward beamed.

"I'll leave it here while I say good-bye to Robert and Sharon," Teresa said. "You can play with it if you like."

She moved out of the way as Carlos supervised the shoving aside of magazines. Uncle Edward placed the house in the cleared space on the table. It fit perfectly.

In his quiet voice, he explained how everything worked, just like he had for her.

Auntie Bee was holding the cloth bag with the drawstring closure that she'd made for the furniture. "Here," she said, handing it to Louise. "These are all the bits and pieces Teresa uses as furniture."

Louise drew the things out of the bag one by one and they all helped place them in the house. While everyone was busy, Teresa slipped away with Jan.

"What about this?" she heard Betty say. Teresa looked back. She was holding up the belt buckle.

"It's the bathtub," Auntie Bee explained.

"Of course!" said Betty.

"There now," said Robert, smacking his hands together. "We'll see you in six months for a checkup and adjustments."

"You make me sound like a car," said Teresa.

"Your leg is a lot like that," said Robert. "We'll be giving you (or it, I should say) a lube and oil job on each of your future visits."

"Have fun this winter with the skating," said Sharon, "It'll be good exercise, but take care. And get in touch right away if you have any problems at all."

Even before she and Jan came back through the glass doors into the waiting room, Teresa could hear the laughter. The log house had never seen such action.

Pipe cleaner people were peeking out the windows and the front door. They straddled the roof and even sat on the chimney.

"Looks like the old woman who lived in a shoe," said Jan.

Teresa stared at the activity. Not one child was sitting alone in the waiting room.

Louise came and stood beside her. "I'll miss you," she whispered. "Thanks for being my friend."

"Let's write to each other," Teresa suggested.

"Oh, yes!" said Louise, slipping something into Teresa's pocket. "I'll write you first. Jan will have your address."

Before Teresa had time to find out what she had given her, Louise took her hand and led her around to the back of the log house. Teresa stared. Pipe cleaner people cooked in the kitchen, sat on the stairs and slept in Tape's and Curly's matchbox beds in the loft.

Auntie Bee looked at her watch. "Teresa, we really must be on our way."

"Louise and I will pack up the furniture, won't we Louise?" said Susan in her usual organizing manner.

Teresa glanced at Uncle Edward with an unspoken question. He gave a slight nod in reply. She reached into her pocket for Curly, and there she was. Louise had kept her promise.

"I'm going to leave the log house," said Teresa. "I'm going to leave it here."

"Oh, Teresa!" said Jan.

"Thank you from all of us," said Susan, and the others echoed her words with their own.

Walking tall and straight, Teresa followed Auntie Bee and Uncle Edward out through the glass doors and back along the crowded hall.

She was leaving one log house, but she was going home to another.

"*Leaving the Log House* fills a void in children's literature around issues of disability.

Teresa's thoughts, feelings and worries are aptly described by the author (as if Teresa were one of my many patients). Her journey of building confidence in herself and in her abilities is a tear jerker! Amputee rehabilitation is not a destination but a journey of building emotional and physical confidence."
— Linda McLaren, BSR (PT) Clinical Resource Physiotherapist — Amputation, GF Strong Rehab Centre

Acknowledgements

For sharing their knowledge, answering my endless questions and giving me guided tours, I would like to thank Linda McLaren, Physiotherapist — Amputation, G.F. Strong Rehab Centre, Vancouver; Anne Rankin, Physiotherapist, BC Children's Hospital, Vancouver; and Bronwyn Booth, Office Manager, John Barber Prosthetics, Vancouver.

Also, many thanks to my editor, Maggie deVries, for her wise advice and gentle guidance. It was a pleasure working with her.

photo by Lesley Gering

Leaving the Log House is Ainslie Manson's tenth book for children and her first novel. The dolls in the story, Tape and Curly, are based on real dolls that Ainslie was given as a child. She is also the author of *House Calls: The true story of a pioneer doctor* (Groundwood, 2001) and *Ballerinas Don't Wear Glasses* (Orca, 2000). Ainslie lives and writes in West Vancouver overlooking the sea.

Juvenile fiction titles from Orca Book Publishers.

THE GRAMMA WAR
Kristin Butcher

CAIRO KELLY AND THE MANN
Kristin Butcher

THE SPY IN THE ALLEY
Melanie Jackson

IN THE CLEAR
Anne Laurel Carter

MYSTERY FROM HISTORY
Dayle Campbell Gaetz

THE GOLD DIGGERS CLUB
Karen Rivers

THE LOKI WOLF
Arthur G. Slade

THE WHITE HORSE TALISMAN
Andrea Spalding

THE BLACK BELT BOOKS:
The Big Show, The Bachelors, One Missing Finger,
Frog Face and the Three Boys
Don Trembath

Call 1-800-210-5277 for a complete catalog.